SPOIL ME, DADDY

ELOUISE EAST

Publisher: Elouise East
Cover Design: Elouise East
Cover photo: prometeus from depositphotos
Editor: Maria Vickers
Beta Readers: Emma Brown, Anna K Neal, Emily Alter

CONTENTS

SPOIL ME, DADDY

DEDICATION

To those who think they are not worthy,
You are.

CHAPTER ONE

ZAIRE

"Yes, of course. Traffic permitting, I'll be there by eight-thirty." Zaire Morgan listened to the caller, nodding. "Sure. Thank you. Bye."

He closed his phone, rubbing his eyes with his free hand as he yawned. He'd been awake for the past hour but, for some reason, could not wake up properly. At least, he now knew which school he was being sent to. It was one of the downsides to working for an agency. He didn't know where he would be sent until around seven in the morning when he received a call with the location and times he was needed. Sometimes, it was a nice school; other times, it was not.

Thankfully, most of the students he met were adorable. He specialised in helping with special educational needs children of any age up to eighteen. There was always plenty of work available for him because there was a serious lack of specialised teaching assistants in the school environment. Unfortunately, the job took a lot of energy and not only physical energy. Guaranteed, by the end of the week, Zaire was exhausted and seriously in need to play.

Stepping into his kitchen, he flicked the kettle on and filled his takeaway mug with coffee, needing a hit of caffeine if he was going to manage it through the last day of the week, then he got into his car and drove to the special needs school. He didn't know which age of children he'd be working with until he got there, so he psyched himself up for anything.

Arriving, he parked his car, picked up his bag of tricks and his coat and headed to the reception desk. As he walked, he slipped his ID card over his head, settling it around his neck. Upon entering, he signed in electronically, a printed ID given to him to add to his current one, and he strode off to the early years' classroom. Today would be a day of fun and games with five- and six-year-olds.

Another unpleasant side effect of working for an agency was that he never managed to create deep, meaningful friendships the way he would if he worked in the same school permanently, but he was getting used to it after a year.

An upside to the job was he could pick and choose when he worked. If he received a call one morning, and he didn't want to work, he was able to decline it with no repercussions. Or at least, no repercussions as long as he didn't do it all the time.

The day passed by as he'd expected it to: playing a variety of games, calming children down, singing, dancing, climbing outside and reading, plus all the toileting and hygiene tasks which were needed. By the time school ended, Zaire was shattered. He bid goodbye to the staff, signed out and dropped into the driver's seat. He rested his head back for a moment, breathing deeply and closing his eyes.

Knowing he would not get better until he got home, Zaire started his car and left. As soon as he arrived, he stripped off his trousers and polo shirt, got into the hottest shower he could stand and washed off the week's work. When he'd wrapped the towel around his waist, he hustled to his bed, where he'd dropped his phone and opened it to Rod's name.

"Hey, I'm heading out tonight. You coming?" Zaire asked without a greeting.

"Nah, man. I've got a party with Delia, haven't I?" Rod was his best friend, had been since university.

Zaire had forgotten. "Alright, no worries. Have a good night."

"Hey, Z?"

"What?"

"Head over to Infinity. They've got a free-for-all night on. You never know what you'll find." Rod chuckled and rang off.

Zaire rolled his eyes. It was a good idea, so he threw his phone back on the bed and strode to his wardrobe. He pulled out a cute red halter-neck top and a black satin skirt. Hanging them on the wardrobe door handles until he needed them, he sashayed over to the drawers, skimming his hands over the contents of the top drawer. Zaire chose black nylon stockings with a black lace suspender belt and matching lace underwear.

He threw the towel to the floor and sat on the bed, placing his feet into the suspenders and sliding them up his legs, settling it nicely on his hips. He repeated the action with the underwear, making sure the clips were underneath. He adjusted his cock to fill the material better and smoothed his hand over the front of his groin, loving the feel of the lace covering him. He sat on the bed again, lifting one foot and sliding the stocking up his calf and thigh until he secured it with the clip from the belt. As he slid the other stocking on, he felt something inside him unclench, something free from within him.

When he was done, he stood in front of the mirror, admiring the way the lace clung to every part of him. He skimmed his hands across his body, feeling more like himself with every passing moment.

He hated having to be so buttoned up, so prim and proper when he went to the schools, but naturally, there'd be outrage if he turned up wearing what he preferred to wear every day. He only had to think about how his dad reacted to know the truth.

Zaire fetched his outfit and slid both items on, once again, admiring the look. Choosing some red three-inch heels—he knew his limitations when walking was involved—he slid them on and sat in front of his mirror. He rarely wore a lot of makeup, usually some subdued eyeshadow and lip gloss, but tonight he needed more. By the time he was done, his amber-coloured eyes popped from his features, his cheekbones were more defined, and his lips looked divine.

Satisfied with his appearance, Zaire grabbed his phone and called for a taxi. Finding his short leather jacket, he checked his social media while he waited. When the horn sounded, he locked up his house and departed for the evening.

He never knew what to expect at these free-for-all events. There was always a mix of kinks milling around each other, and it wasn't always easy to find someone with the same kink as he had. Despite that, he was excited to let go.

When the taxi deposited him outside the club, he thanked him and headed towards the building, the bass pounding into the night, even through the closed doors. Infinity had been open for several years and catered to many people. There was a membership section to the club as well as a public side. Zaire couldn't afford to pay to be a member, so had to settle with public events like these.

Music blasted his eardrums as he entered, and he strolled towards the kiosk to pay his entry fee. He swapped his coat for a ticket, which he slipped into a discreet pocket of his skirt, along with his phone. He thanked the staff member and waved his way into the club, heading straight for the bar for a stiff drink.

As he arrived, a gap opened, and he slid into it before anyone else could take it, although someone bumped into him.

"Sorry, sweetheart." A muscular guy squeezed Zaire's arm and shuffled on his way.

Zaire rolled his eyes before turning his attention to the bartender. When the guy moved closer, Zaire shouted his order to him, receiving a shout in his ear afterwards.

"Hey! Wait your turn like everyone else."

Zaire twisted his head to an older man who stood beside him. "If you wait, you'll be here for hours. Shout, and you get their attention. Suck it up." He returned to the bartender who had arrived with Zaire's drink, and Zaire quickly waved his card over the machine to pay. "Thanks." He nodded to the bartender and turned back to the guy. "See? If I were you, I'd shout. Loud."

He pivoted on his heels and sashayed over to the dance floor. The problem with the public area of Infinity was the deafeningly loud music, whereas, for the members-only section, it was a lot more subdued. He'd never experienced it himself, but he'd been told when he'd inquired about the membership benefits. Maybe in a couple of years, he'd be able to save enough for a membership, but as it was, he was paying off his car and a mortgage, so money was tight, despite how much he worked.

Rolling his head on his neck to loosen the muscles, Zaire studied the patrons of the club. From what he could see, there were Doms and subs, puppy play, a Mummy and her boy, master and slave to name a few. When they said free-for-all, they really meant it. What Zaire couldn't see was anyone looking like a Daddy. His shoulders slumped, and he blew out a breath. Why was it so difficult to find what he wanted? Soon, he would need to take an ad out to get people to interview for the position. He chuckled at that. It might be quite entertaining to see who turned up to such an advertisement.

"Hey, gorgeous. Are you here with someone or searching for someone?" a voice purred in Zaire's ear.

Glancing over his shoulder, he saw a tall black guy with huge muscles whose demeanour screamed Master. Zaire smiled and whirled around to greet the guy. He never ignored people who approached him; it was a social nicety. "Hey! I am looking for someone, but I have a feeling you're not going to be what I need, sir."

"So polite. Are you sure?"

"May I ask a question, sir?" Despite not wanting what this Master was so obviously offering, Zaire knew to treat all dominants with respect. Disrespecting others got people kicked out of the club quicker than they could apologise.

"Go ahead."

"Are you a Daddy?"

The Master smiled gently. "No, sweet boy. I know there are a couple here tonight, though I don't know if they have boys themselves." He slid a finger down Zaire's cheek. "Thank you for checking with me. Good luck tonight."

"Thank you, sir. And you."

Zaire watched as the guy moved through the crowd before returning his gaze to the masses, trying to find those elusive Daddies.

After spending a couple of hours circling the hordes, finding a Daddy who, unfortunately, already had a boy and drinking some more but not enough to be drunk, Zaire had decided enough was enough. He stood at the bar, which was not as busy as earlier, and requested one more drink while he waited for his taxi to arrive.

As he brought the tumbler to his mouth, someone bumped into his back, spilling the drink on his shirt and skirt.

"What the fuck! Watch where you're going! It's not like I'm difficult to see wearing a bright red satin shirt! Fucking thing is ruined now." Zaire plucked the wet fabric away from his skin and grimaced. He would be stinking of whiskey for his journey home, and to top it all, his favourite top was toast.

"Sorry. I really am. Let me help…" the guy tried dabbling at the fabric with a napkin, but Zaire batted his hands away.

Zaire sighed. "Leave it. Just be more careful around other people. I'm outta here."

Spinning around, he elbowed his way through the crowds to the entrance, pulling out a wet wardrobe ticket to retrieve his coat before exiting in the warm night. Staring up at the sky, he exhaled, shaking his head. Not only had the night been a total bust, but he'd ruined an outfit. He needed to sleep this night off and start fresh in the morning.

"That was a bit harsh, wasn't it?"

Zaire spun around, gripping the edges of his leather jacket as he identified the guy as being the older man from earlier, who'd called him out for pushing in at the bar.

"What's it to you?"

"I thought the idea was to be polite to people." He was stood outside the entrance doors but close enough Zaire didn't have to strain to hear him.

"Maybe so. But sometimes you also need to tell someone when they're being an ass," Zaire countered.

The guy raised his eyebrows. "Is that so?"

Zaire raised his chin. "Yeah."

"In which case…" he paused, "you were an asshole."

Stunned, Zaire blinked at the guy. He couldn't believe he'd been called out on his behaviour when it was the other guy's fault for knocking into him. He told the guy his thoughts.

"But you could have been nicer about it. He did apologise, and he did try to help clean up. Regardless of how it happened, the behaviour afterwards should have shown he was contrite. Your punishment didn't fit his crime."

The words "punishment" and "crime" wound Zaire up tighter, especially as there was no release in sight. But the guy had a point. "Shit," he muttered, staring at his shoe as he swivelled one foot on his heel.

"Maybe you need to think about your actions before reacting to outside influences."

With the reprimand, the guy whirled and headed back into the club. Under other circumstances, Zaire would've been interested in him, especially the confident air around him. He could almost feel the guy's beard and moustache, the same light-brown colour as his hair, sliding against his skin. Zaire watched until the door closed behind him, the outburst of music muting once more. "Fuck!"

A horn made him flinch, and he twisted around to see a taxi waiting at the kerb. He stalked over, checking the number plate and name with what he had on his phone before entering and slamming the door behind him.

"Rough night?" the driver asked.

Zaire snorted without humour. "Could've been better."

"Ah, there's always tomorrow."

And there was the problem. There was an infinite amount of tomorrows, but Zaire was fed up with waiting for his tomorrow to arrive. He wanted to share his life with someone who would take care of him and help him reduce the stresses in his life. And finding someone would be one less stress for him.

CHAPTER TWO

AARON

He checked the figures once more and rubbed at the back of his neck. Regardless of how many times he reread it, he could see the special needs department was suffering from being understaffed. Aaron needed to bring in more people but also didn't have a huge budget to do so. The best idea would be to get an experienced agency member and see how they go. If they were good, he could offer them a job, reducing the outlay of using an agency—after having to pay the agency exit fee, that was.

Standing, he stuck his head outside his office door and asked Pamela to come in. As he returned to his desk, they entered, sitting opposite him. Pamela had been a fantastic help for him while he was finding his feet in this new position, going above and beyond what was required of them, such as being in the office at seven in the morning when it should have been eight.

"How can I help, Mr Brown?"

"Please. I keep telling you, call me, Aaron. Especially when there is no one else around." He smiled to lessen the sting of potentially offending them. "I need a list of agencies where we could get some staff experienced with special needs. Being new to the area, I don't know which ones you use."

"Sure thing. I can get you the list. If I recall, there are five or six we have used in the past."

"That would be great. Thanks, Pamela."

They left and, within minutes, returned with a list. Thanking them again, he was left alone. Picking up the phone, he dialled the first number. After going through what he wanted, they said they didn't have anyone available for that day, but they would tomorrow. Aaron thanked them and agreed to keep their school on the agency's books. He bid goodbye and dialled another.

"Yes, we have a couple of teaching assistants available today. Thinking about what you wanted, you probably need our most experienced. He has many years' experience but has only been temping with us for the last year. He comes highly recommended and has been requested the most out of all of our staff."

Aaron knew the agency would increase an assistant's abilities to make sure they get a foot in the door at the school, but he was also desperate. "Fantastic. If we could have him, if he's available, and two others if you have them, we will see how things go from there."

"No problem at all. I will get on the phone to them now and let you know if less than three can make it."

"Thank you."

Aaron put the phone down and sat back in his chair with a sigh. When he had first taken on the role, he had been excited about it, but as soon as the previous principal had left—early and without warning—Aaron had felt like he was drowning. He knew as soon as the place was running smoothly, everything would be fine, but at the moment, he wondered why he'd even agreed to the job.

"Pamela?"

They poked their head through his door.

"We have three agency staff coming in today. One is apparently very experienced. At some point this afternoon, I'd like some feedback from the teacher as to how good he is, please."

"Sure thing. Where do you want him?"

"In the class where an experienced special needs teaching assistant is most needed."

"Year one, then. I'll ask Uma to come and see you before the end of school."

Aaron nodded. "Great, thanks." He scratched his nails across his beard and wished he could head to the gym for a workout, the stress of the day was already getting to him, and it was only seven-forty.

Leaning forward again, he refocused on the paper-work, hoping things would change sooner rather than later.

↔

At lunchtime, he ate his couscous and salad at his desk so he could continue his work. He didn't feel like he was making any headway, but he must've been. His school was a mixed ability school, which meant it included all children regardless of their protected characteristics or special requirements. He didn't see why he couldn't provide what each child needed with a bit of research and funding. It was the funding that was the problem. He'd argued with the education committee many times already about the need for more cash, but as usual, money was what made the world go round.

Pamela brought him a cup of coffee, for which he was eternally grateful, and slipped out of his office again.

Aaron rested back in his chair with another sigh, probably the fiftieth that day, and thought back to the previous Friday night. He'd gone out with Nora, his best friend of thirty-odd years. They had met in secondary school in Lincoln, and after college, Nora had moved with her then-boyfriend to Cambridge. After Aaron's departure from his previous role, Nora had suggested he relocate. He loved Cambridge, always had whenever he had visited her, and more so now he lived there.

Friday had been the first time in several weeks when he'd had enough energy to venture out. Nora had told him about a free-for-all night at one of the clubs, and as she and her now-husband, Geoff, were in a Mistress and puppy relationship, it allowed Aaron and Nora to go together rather than have to split up as they had to occasionally. Apparently, some clubs thought Daddies and Mummies, and Masters and Mistresses shouldn't mix, which was a rather silly notion, which was, thankfully, not seconded by many places.

He'd been talking to Nora at the bar, waiting to be served when a guy shouted his order near his ear. Despite the pounding music, the voice was piercing and had Aaron wincing and twisting to tell the guy to wait his turn. The guy, dressed in an eye-catching red halter-neck, gave him the cold hard facts as he'd believed them to be and promptly received his drink within minutes. Giving Aaron a final word, he'd sashayed off, his hips and skirt swaying with the beat of the music.

After the guy had left, Aaron had raised his eyebrows at Nora and shrugged, then shouted their order to the bartender. Several minutes later, their drinks were in front of them, and he'd wished he could thank the guy.

Later that night, he'd seen the same guy give a dressing down to someone who had bumped into him. Okay, his perfectly fitted clothing had possibly been ruined by whiskey, especially as he heard the word satin being bantered around, but the accident-prone guy didn't deserve the words thrown his way.

When the guy had muttered and left, Aaron couldn't help but follow. As he saw the guy stare at the sky, words escaped before he realised what he was going to say. His tongue reprimanded the guy's response, and apart from the initial push back, the guy had taken the slap on the wrist well. It hadn't been Aaron's place, but he couldn't help but make the guy aware his actions had been way over the top.

If he had been his boy, he would've been spanked and denied orgasms and Aaron's cock until Aaron believed he understood. The guy hadn't been, though, and a verbal reprimand was the best he could do.

Aaron shook his head, knowing he needed to find himself a boy, or someone, to hook up with. He struggled to find someone who pushed his buttons because he was more attracted to a person's personality than their looks, and many people hid behind a social curtain instead of being themselves. But maybe getting laid would clear his brain.

When Pamela knocked on his door that afternoon with a report from Uma, Aaron was grateful for the interruption.

"Uma says the sub," Aaron's heart rate increased at that word even though the meaning was different, "is amazing, and can she have him forever?" Pamela smirked as they stood there.

Aaron chuckled. "Okay. Could you see if the guy is around so I can have a chat with him, please?"

"Sure thing, boss."

Ten minutes later, Pamela knocked again. "Are you okay to see him now?"

"Sure."

Aaron closed the file he had been working on and stood from his desk as the guy walked in. As Aaron's gaze lifted to the guy's face, he stalled, eyebrows raising. This should be interesting.

"Thank you, Pamela."

They closed the door behind them. As silence descended, Aaron studied him. The black styled hair; warm, amber-coloured eyes; soft-looking, clean-shaven skin and full lips holding a hint of a smirk.

"We meet again…" Aaron held his hand out as he paused for the guy to finish Aaron's sentence with his name.

"Zaire…Morgan." A hand clasped his in a strong but not challenging grip.

"Aaron Brown. Please take a seat."

They both sat, eyes locked as they sized each other up.

"I apologise for the way I behaved on Friday."

Aaron wasn't sure who was more shocked by Zaire's apology: him or Zaire. He saw Zaire clench his jaw and fidget in his seat, so Aaron took pity on him.

"Thank you. I appreciate you saying that."

Zaire snorted. "I wish I could say it was a one-time thing," he rubbed his fingers across his mouth, "but thinking back on previous nights out, it probably wasn't. I can be…" Zaire paused, his focus moving off to Aaron's right as he seemed to search for a word.

"Temperamental?" Aaron supplied.

Zaire flicked his gaze back to Aaron and laughed. "Yeah, that pretty much covers it. But only outside of work." He held his hand palm forward, letting Aaron know he was serious. "Within work, I am reliable and respectable. I keep the two sides separate."

"So, I've heard. You come highly recommended, Zaire. I don't think those words will inflate your ego any more than it is already," Aaron declared with a smirk.

Zaire's lips twitched. "I come wherever I'm commanded to."

Aaron raised his eyebrow. Did the guy seriously flirt with him?

"Sorry." Zaire linked his fingers in his lap and crossed his legs, gaze dropping.

The undeniable submission Zaire showed sparked a flint in Aaron's chest, and he schooled his features. "No, you're not."

Zaire's gaze rose for a second, a twinkle in his eyes until he dropped his gaze once more. "No, I'm not," he whispered.

"You said you were reliable and respectable. If I can ensure you'll leave the innuendos at the entrance to the school, I would love to have you back again. What do you say?"

Aaron watched as Zaire's jaw tightened again, and he swallowed. "I believe I would enjoy working here."

"That's good news. I'll speak to the agency and request you stay with us for the next two weeks. If you appear to fit within the team, I might extend a permanent job offer, if you'd be interested."

Zaire's expression brightened. "I would. Thank you."

"Don't thank me yet. Thank me if I offer you the job." Aaron grinned.

Smiling, Zaire stood, holding out his hand once more. "Regardless. Thank you. For today and last Friday."

"You're very welcome, Zaire. Just remember what I said."

Their hands clasped for longer than was necessary, and when they parted, Zaire's fingertips slid across Aaron's palm.

"See you tomorrow."

Zaire exited the office, and Aaron breathed deeply before picking up the phone and calling the agency. After explaining his terms, they agreed on a two-week employment for Zaire. Aaron didn't mention anything about the possibility of a job at the end of it. That would be discussed if Zaire behaved.

Aaron thought about Zaire's demeanour as he'd sat in front of him and from Friday night. There was no doubt Zaire had confidence in spades, but he appeared to need reining in a bit. Friday night showed his ego might be a problem, but if he was true to his word and kept the two sides to himself separate, he'd fit nicely. Aaron was concerned about the separation aspect. Surely, it wasn't healthy to keep aspects of his personality in different compartments.

He frowned as he tried to figure out how Zaire worked. The side of Zaire he'd seen on Friday was brash, egocentric, graceful and sexy. Today, he'd seen buttoned-up, clean-shaven, confident with some uneasiness if Aaron wasn't mistaken. Which was the real Zaire Morgan?

Shaking his head, he returned his attention to his workload. Then, hesitating, grabbed his phone.

I need relief. Which club or bar is the best choice for tonight?

He sent the text to Nora, knowing she would reply as soon as she could. Naturally, having lived here for thirty years, she knew the place better than he did and had been on the scene longer. He picked up a file and opened it, trying hard to concentrate on what was inside.

A knock sounded.

"Come in."

Pamela smiled. "It's time for assembly."

"Okay. Thanks. I didn't realise the time."

"No problem. It's what I'm here for." Pamela grinned and left the office, leaving the door open, presumably to remind him to get his ass up.

Dropping his phone into a drawer and locking it, he stood, heading to the hall ready to give his end of the day assembly. They alternated when they had assemblies and didn't have them every day like a lot of schools did. He found children fidgeted a lot the longer they had to sit still, so he had introduced a few changes.

He waited at the front of the hall, pacing, as the children entered, some smiling at him, some shy. He crouched to make himself smaller, so he didn't appear as scary. One of the first changes he had made was to reverse how the classes sat. Usually, the youngest children sat at the front and the oldest at the back. Aaron had read some research once that younger children would benefit from being further away from a person they may be frightened of, especially if he was pacing in front of them all the time. It had the added effect of making the older kids sit closer to him, where he could see the troublemakers.

Once everyone had settled in, he greeted them, "Good afternoon, students."

"Good afternoon, Mr Brown. Good afternoon, teachers."

"Thank you. Firstly, can I say you are all looking very smart today." He caught the gaze of a few students and smiled. "Today, we are going to talk about books."

As Aaron carried on talking about favourite books and calling on children to talk about theirs, he tried to decide if the two other changes he had made were making a difference. Assemblies now only happened on Monday and Wednesday afternoons and a Friday morning. And in the middle of each assembly was an active session.

"Right. You know what time it is now. Everyone, stand up." Aaron indicated for the piano teacher to get ready. "Remember, please think about where your feet and hands are. We don't want other children getting hurt if you are too close to them. Go!"

He watched as all the pupils jumped, hopped, danced, shimmied, and whatever else they could think of as the music played. After a three-minute burst, the music ended, and all the children dropped to their bottoms.

"Fantastic work, kids. Now, if you can sit nicely again for me, we will have our story."

Aaron switched on the projector, and the story's pictures filled the wall behind him. As he read through the book in his hand, he scanned the children, seeing them hardly fidgeting at all. Maybe it did work. More research had shown that children found it physically painful to sit still for any length of time, so he'd introduced the physical burst to allow them to shake it off, in the theory they would be able to sit still again afterwards.

Time would tell if it worked.

As he finished the story, he caught Zaire's eye. Aaron couldn't decipher the expression on his face. It was almost as if he was shocked but not. Focusing back on the children, he bid them a good day. After they left the hall, Aaron found his way back to his office, checking his phone immediately.

The best place would be Infinity, again. The membership section is the best bet, but I don't know if you want to do that yet. Otherwise, stay in the public section and see what's there. Any other clubs on a Monday aren't the best idea for Daddies. X

Aaron exhaled and nodded. He was heading back to the club. He needed to scratch this itch, desperately.

CHAPTER THREE

ZAIRE

He couldn't believe the headteacher was the guy who'd told him off on Friday. What were the chances? Zaire smiled, recalling Mr Brown's well-tailored suit and a tie that matched his dark-brown eyes. He was gorgeous. Zaire could admit the guy ticked all of Zaire's boxes. If only he could be a Daddy. The guy must have some kink or fetish to have been in the club on Friday, but what was anyone's guess. He had been with a woman, so he probably wasn't even gay. Zaire tilted his head. Aaron had rebuffed his flirtatious attempts, so he probably was straight.

Driving home, he thought about what it would be like to head to the same place of work every day. The school today had been a breath of fresh air. The teacher had explained the headteacher—Aaron—was moving with the times and willing to listen to their opinions. It wasn't often you found a place like that. If what Uma said was true, he'd love to work there.

The agency rang as he was plating his dinner, and he answered immediately.

"Zaire. I have a proposition for you."

"Go on."

"The school today would like you to stay for two weeks. Are you happy to?"

"Sure, that's fine."

"He didn't say the words, but it might turn into something permanent."

Zaire could almost hear the clink of money in the guy's voice as he thought about the severance fee the school would have to pay if Zaire went permanent. Every company had to pay a lot to take a staff member off the agency's books.

"Maybe. But thanks. Yes. It would be nice to be in the same place for a short while."

"Fantastic. I will leave a message for the head saying you agreed. I'll speak to you at the end of the week."

Zaire clicked off the phone and sighed with relief. He hadn't been lying. Being in one place would be nice but being close to Aaron might be more than he could handle.

Aaron had been amazing in the assembly that afternoon, and the children responded to him. Zaire smiled as he remembered watching Aaron jumping up and down in the physical session. Only a couple of the other teachers had taken part.

For once, Zaire was looking forward to working.

<—————————>

Zaire entered the bar with Rod near the end of the week and wished Rod had chosen somewhere else. Infinity was packed, and though Zaire usually didn't mind crowds, he was ready for an easy night out with a friend rather than the happy ending type of night Rod had in mind. He supposed it wouldn't hurt to get laid, reducing his stress levels would be beneficial, but he couldn't get up the energy for the chase.

He also wasn't sure if he was likely to bump into Aaron there, too.

Climbing onto a handily vacated seat when he arrived at the bar, Zaire tried to converse with Rod, who was already searching the sea of people for his conquest.

"I'm assuming things with Delia aren't good." Zaire didn't understand their open relationship, but it wasn't up to him to understand it. He supported Rod when he needed it and hoped things didn't go wrong for him.

"She's being difficult again. I told her where I was going, so it's not like she doesn't know what might happen." Rod's gaze searched the masses as he spoke.

Zaire couldn't imagine sleeping with someone else when the perfect person was waiting at home for him. It didn't sit right with him, but it wasn't his relationship, so he had no right to a say in it. "God, I need a drink. What do you want?"

"Beer, please."

"Two beers and a whiskey, please!" Zaire yelled to the bartender. As he waited, he spun the cardboard coaster advertising a beer brand and yawned. He shouldn't even be here.

"You look like you need a drink."

Zaire turned to face a slim guy with shoulder-length dark hair, bright green eyes and a wicked grin.

"I don't know if it's a good thing or not." He raised his eyebrows in question.

"It's a good thing because it means I can ask you if I can buy you a drink to help."

"I've got one on its way, but maybe next time." Zaire liked the guy's confidence, and his appearance didn't hurt either.

"Sure. I'm happy to hang around until you finish the one you have." The guy held out his hand. "Name's Griff.

"Zaire."

When his drinks arrived, he passed a beer to Rod, placed the whiskey in front of him and slid the other beer over to Griff.

"I thought I was buying you a drink."

"Both of these were for me, but if you help me drink that one, you'll get to buy me a drink a lot faster." Zaire winked and slammed the whiskey back.

Griff chuckled. Zaire saw it in his shoulders rather than heard it, and he watched unabashedly as Griff lifted the bottle to his lips and drank, his Adam's apple repeatedly bobbing as he swallowed. Zaire had not planned on finding a date tonight. He'd decided to go home and sleep as soon as Rod had found someone, but Griff seemed like too good a choice to pass up.

"I love what you're wearing," Griff whispered in Zaire's ear. "You look so fucking sexy."

Zaire grinned. "Thanks. I feel it."

He had chosen tights under three-quarter length teal-coloured trousers and a black off the shoulder chenille jumper. Comfortable but stylish—his own style; he loved mixing it up. His makeup was barely there but with a shimmer to his skin.

Griff's gaze slid over his body again, appreciation evident in his eyes.

A beer bottle slammed down next to him, making him jump. "I'm out," Rod said, and Zaire turned to watch as he stalked towards a woman who eyed him like her next meal.

"A friend of yours?"

"Yeah, best friend. I was the wingman tonight."

"Looks like you both got lucky."

Zaire snorted. "You're full of yourself, aren't you?"

"Would you prefer me to be meek and timid?"

"No. It's refreshing."

Griff leaned forward. "Would you be happy to continue this somewhere else?"

"What about the drink?"

"You can have a drink if you want it." Griff shrugged. "Or we can skip it this time."

Tilting his head, Zaire made a decision. An orgasm or two would help him sleep, even more than whiskey would—without the headache in the morning. At least, in theory.

"We can skip, but I'm going to be honest with you." Griff nodded for him to continue. "We can go to my place, but you're not staying over. Agreed?"

"That's fair. A mutually beneficial transaction and I'm gone."

"Happy with that?" Zaire wanted Griff's word. Nobody ever stayed overnight at his house. He made sure of it.

"Yes."

Zaire pulled out his phone and ordered a taxi. "Come on." Zaire hopped off the stool and headed to the exit, not bothering to check if Griff was following. He thought he saw Aaron at one point, but when he turned his head, it wasn't him. He was either imagining it or the guy walked fast.

As they waited outside, Zaire took stock of the guy as he messaged Rod to let him know he was taking someone home. Griff seemed honest, but everyone had to be careful, regardless. He lifted his phone to Griff and asked if he could take a photo. Griff looked confused but agreed. Zaire snapped it and sent it with the message to Rod before explaining to Griff.

"I don't know you. If you're a serial killer, my friend now has your picture to give to the police. I'm more inclined to believe you aren't as you let me take your photo in the first place." Zaire smiled at the bemusement on Griff's face. "Although you could quite as easily kill me and go for Rod, I suppose."

Griff burst out laughing. "You're something else. I like it."

"I know what I want, and I know how to be safe. What more can I say?" He was saved from saying anything else by the taxi arriving.

Once they were settled inside Zaire's house, Griff stepped forward. "What do you want me to be?"

Zaire studied Griff's expression, seeing it open and true. "Daddy," he whispered.

Griff smiled and kissed him.

⟵―――――――――⟶

Zaire's ass smarted as he sat cross-legged on the floor with a child as they prepared for the sensology session. This was one of Zaire's favourites. Five children and three staff members sat or laid on the floor of the spacious room. Each session was based on a different theme. That day, it was The Greatest Showman, and the idea was with each song on the album, staff would use and help the children to use different props to explore the music. Zaire had a box next to him with the props for the child he was helping, and a piece of paper detailing what the recommended activities were.

When the music started, Zaire began brushing a feather over the child's arm, smiling when the child moved their face towards Zaire and grinned. This was one of the most rewarding jobs in the world as far as Zaire was concerned. Children were precious gifts who, hopefully, knew little of how harsh the world could be.

Zaire hoped he would get on well at this school. It would be great if he didn't have to worry about where he would end up being sent every morning. Having one place of work was more convenient, and this school was almost on his doorstep, which he couldn't have chosen better. He hoped his attraction to the headteacher wouldn't prove his undoing.

Aaron had been professional, even when Zaire pushed things and flirted, which he should not have done. It was hardly professional to flirt with your potential boss-to-be. He shook his head at himself. He was an idiot.

After the session had finished, he helped return the children to the classrooms and sat, wincing, with some craft items to help a child make a crown.

"Are you okay, Zaire?" Uma asked, resting a hand on his shoulder. "I've seen you grimace a few times today."

Zaire told himself not to blush. "I pulled a muscle yesterday; whenever I sit or stand, it smarts."

"Ah, not good." She sat beside him. "I know you've only been here a week, but how are you finding it?"

Zaire smiled. "I love it here. I would like to be able to stay for longer."

"Well, we have you for at least another week, Aaron told me, maybe more if everything goes well."

His stomach fluttered at Aaron's name, and he admonished himself silently. "Yes, hopefully."

"I'm glad you're enjoying it. Let me know if you have any problems or questions, okay?"

"Sure thing."

Uma smiled and headed off when she was called away. Zaire wanted to stay there. Everyone seemed great and willing to go to great lengths to help the children. At least in this class, they seemed to. He didn't have any experience with the other classes. Returning to his job as a crown maker, he helped the child glue enough gems on to light a disco ball until they deemed it fit for a king. Once the child had the crown on their head, a cape around their shoulders and a cardboard sword by their side, they knighted Zaire as a soldier, and Zaire received his own cardboard sword.

The rest of the day was interspersed between being a soldier, a ghost and a monster, depending on which child wanted his attention. Zaire had great fun.

Striding to his car, he checked his phone, seeing Rod had messaged him.

Delia is pissed at me. We had a huge argument this morning about yesterday.

Zaire rolled his eyes. If Rod couldn't see what was right in front of him, he didn't deserve Delia. He couldn't remember the last time Rod had mentioned Delia going out and finding someone from outside their relationship. In fact, it had been months, and Zaire had been able to see Delia was falling more and more for his clueless best friend. He thought it was time to let Rod in on some hard truths.

When was the last time Delia went out and had sex with someone other than you?

Several minutes later, after he'd got semi-comfortable in the driver's seat, he received a reply.

What does that mean?

Answer the question.

I don't know. A few weeks?

Try a few months. Do you think there is something you need to talk about? If Delia isn't happy about the way your relationship is now, you need to talk and figure it out. Or you are going to lose the best thing that ever happened to you.

There was no reply straight away, so Zaire drove home, hearing his phone chime after around ten minutes. He didn't check it until he parked in his driveway.

How would I know?

Know what?

If she wanted to change how things were?

ASK HER!!!!

Zaire entered his house, throwing his keys and phone onto the table before hanging up his coat and resting his bag underneath. He kicked off his shoes, picking up his phone when it buzzed.

Fine, I will.

Good, let me know how it goes.

Zaire climbed the stairs, undoing the buttons of his shirt as he went, eager to relax and return to his home self. Stripping completely, he threw his clothes in the wash basket and strode to his drawers. He riffled through, finding a pair of lace shorts and pulled them on, sighing in contentment when they were in place. He grabbed his satin robe and wrapped it around him. It was his security blanket.

Muscles releasing the tension from the day, he danced his way back down the stairs and made himself a cup of warm milk and headed to the living room. The cup was placed on the small side table and a timer set on his phone before he pulled out a blue box from the cupboard. Opening it up, Zaire sighed and removed his cars and building blocks. Then he lost himself in the world of racing.

When his alarm sounded, he pushed up from his stomach and tidied away his toys with reluctance. He would've loved to stay playing for longer, but he had to eat. If he had a Daddy, he wouldn't always have to stop to make dinner. He wanted to share his life with someone who understood what it was he wanted. It was so hard to find, though. He wished Aaron had been a Daddy. Zaire could see Aaron being an amazingly caring Daddy for a boy.

Sighing, he put the box away and returned to reality.

CHAPTER FOUR

AARON

Aaron had seen Zaire several times throughout the two weeks. He had purposefully sought him out to see what kind of job he was doing, and putting it mildly, he was great at it. Zaire was patient with the children, a quick learner when it came to new rules or new children, and everyone seemed to adore him.

On the Friday of Zaire's last trial day, Aaron asked Pamela to request Zaire join him in his office. As he waited, Aaron had mixed feelings. One was a professional opinion; the other was purely selfish reasons.

The professional side of things would be discussed in the office. As for the personal feelings…Aaron had more than liked what he'd seen of Zaire, both from the night out and from working there. There seemed to be two sides to Zaire, and Aaron itched to be the one to help Zaire merge the two into one whole personality. He could tell from seeing both sides of him that Zaire kept his private side private and on the down-low from his work side, which he had every right to. But Aaron could see it was wearing on him. He was sure it was one of the reasons for the outburst he'd witnessed at the club.

Aaron would love nothing more than to take Zaire apart and build him back up again into someone Zaire could live with. At the moment, a part of Zaire was hiding no matter what role he was in.

A knock sounded, and he allowed Zaire entry.

"Thanks for coming. Take a seat." Aaron tried to brush away his personal thoughts and focus on the professional.

"I'm always happy to come," Zaire said, gaze demurely dropped away from Aaron's face.

Aaron cleared his throat, refusing to rise to the bait. "I've heard feedback from the teachers you've worked alongside and seen you working myself, and I'm impressed, Zaire. You do a fantastic job."

A flush worked its way onto Zaire's cheeks, and Aaron could see he was trying to withhold a smile, but he could see the sparkle in Zaire's eyes at the acknowledgement of his ability. "Thank you."

"Do you enjoy working with children?"

Zaire's eyebrows lowered. "Of course, I do. I wouldn't be here, otherwise."

Aaron tilted his head back and forth. "Not everyone who comes into these jobs do it because they enjoy it. Sometimes they do it because it's the only thing available to them at the time. I wanted to make sure you were from the first group."

Crossing his legs and threading his fingers together in his lap, Zaire answered, "I love helping the kids. All children, regardless of who they are, have so much love to give people. Others need to stop and see it for what it is."

"Which is?" Aaron asked when Zaire didn't continue.

"Unconditional. Children don't like you because you give them things, they love you because you are there for them, you spend time with them."

Aaron smiled, nodding slowly. "I knew you loved children. I wanted to check."

Zaire snorted. "Check what?"

"Whether you'd be honest with me." Aaron's gaze bored into Zaire's as something passed between them until Aaron cleared his throat again and looked down at his paperwork. "I would like to offer you a position here."

"Thank you. Can I think about it?"

Aaron raised his eyebrows, surprised by Zaire's answer. He thought it would be an immediate agreement. "Of course. If you could let me know as soon as you can, I'd appreciate it. If your answer is no, I need to find a suitable replacement."

"You wouldn't keep me on under the agency?" Zaire asked.

"Unfortunately, not. Funding only lasts so long, and I have enough for short term agency staff, but in the long run, I need to find a permanent member of staff."

"Understandable. Could I let you know on Monday?"

"That would be great. You would be a great addition to the school, Zaire." Aaron smiled at him as he stood, holding out his hand.

Zaire grinned and gripped Aaron's hand. "I know."

Aaron narrowed his eyes on Zaire, silently reprimanding him for his egotistical remark, and receiving widened eyes and a dropped gaze from Zaire. Aaron let go of Zaire's hand, making sure to slide his fingers along Zaire's palm as they slipped apart.

"Have a good weekend, Zaire."

Zaire's gaze locked with his, momentarily. "Thank you, sir."

Aaron clenched his jaw against the words he wanted to say, mainly, "Those words sound perfect on your lips," but he refrained…barely.

The rest of the day was uneventful. Aaron had plenty of paperwork to get through, and his head was pounding by the time everyone had gone home. Packing up the things he would take home to do over the weekend, Aaron switched off his computer and left the building, knowing the cleaning crew would lock everything up at the end of the evening.

After the short drive home, Aaron yawned and dropped his bag in his office before heading for the shower. As much as he'd prefer to faceplant on the bed, he had agreed to go to Infinity for Daddy night. Nora wouldn't be in attendance, but she had arranged for a friend to meet him there, so he wasn't on his own all night. It was her way of pushing him towards what he wanted without arranging a blind date. The only reason he'd agreed was her friend was a Daddy, too, so Aaron knew they wouldn't be leaving together; therefore, not a date.

He didn't hold out much hope because boys were difficult to find at the best of times. But finding one whose needs fit with Aaron's was almost impossible.

Zaire's face flitted through his mind, and Aaron remembered what he'd been wearing the first night Aaron had seen him. He had wondered what Zaire had been wearing underneath, and if it was what he thought it was—wished it was.

Aaron's boy needed to have a love of lace, satin and silk. He loved nothing more than seeing his boy pottering around the house while wearing nothing but lacy underwear, a silk chemise, or even knowing it was underneath their clothing. He needed as close to a twenty-four-seven Daddy and boy relationship, something that was not always possible.

Feeling his body reacting to the visions, Aaron switched the shower on and stepped inside, his cock twitching as the water hit the swollen length. He wet his hair to cool him and gripped his shaft. Knowing it would make his life more difficult when he saw Zaire every day—if he took the job—didn't stop Aaron from thinking about the guy.

Using the tips of his fingers, he played with his foreskin, rubbing back and forth until his cock was rock hard, then he wrapped his hand around it and stroked to images of Zaire dressed in lace underwear and the tights he had worn the first night. Aaron imagined running his hands underneath the skirt, smoothing his hands over the fabric, turning Zaire and bending him over the stool and flipping the skirt up his back to expose his ass encased in lace and the gap where Aaron's cock would so rightly fit. As he took Zaire, he would be able to run his hands across the satin fabric and the naked skin of Zaire's back, feeling the sweat build up there as he pounded into him.

Aaron slapped a hand against the wet tiles, thrusting his hips as his hand gripped his dick firmer. Keeping his hand still, he clenched his ass muscles and snapped his hips repeatedly as he fucked his hand, imagining Zaire was in front of him.

"Fuck! Yes! Ah!" Aaron growled loudly as he came, spurting his release over the tiles. He panted as he rested his forehead against the cool surface, the water beating down on his back. When his legs became stronger again, he unlocked his knees and stood tall, sticking his head under the water again.

If things had been tenuous before due to his attraction to Zaire, now he'd made his life ten thousand times more complicated. He'd have to hope he could have a conversation with Zaire without remembering what he'd stroked off to.

Sighing, he finished washing up and dried off, heading for his wardrobe. Aaron needed to be comfortable. So, he went with his usual outfit: well-worn blue jeans and an emerald green shirt with the top buttons undone. The first time he'd been at the club with Nora, he'd worn a suit and had regretted it the moment he'd arrived. This time, he was determined to be himself. As he told his boys so often, there was no point pretending to be something you're not.

Sliding his wallet and phone into the pockets of his jeans, he headed to the kitchen and grabbed a coffee to go. He was driving because he'd have transport should he find someone to share the evening with. Picking up his keys, he locked the door behind him and strode to his car. He had no idea what the night would bring, but the worst would be a new friend within the community. No one could ask for more.

◄─────────►

Two hours later, Aaron wished he'd stayed at home. Cord was nice enough, and Aaron would be happy to spend time with him, but there were no boys available. All of them already had Daddies, and that was the problem Aaron found everywhere. Boys were hard to find.

"Is it always like this?" Aaron asked Cord when he returned with some beers.

"Like what?"

"More Daddies than boys? I know it was where I used to live, but I thought it was just there."

"It's been like this for as long as I can remember. Available boys come in on rare occasions, and when they do, they're inundated with choices." Cord sat back in his chair, lifting the beer to his mouth.

Aaron shook his head. "No wonder we can't find anyone. We probably scare them all away."

"There is that. Some of these guys have been single for years. It's so difficult, but what can we do? We are who we are."

Aaron had nothing to say to those whispered words because it was so true. He wiped a hand over his mouth and decided to go home.

"I'm going—" He stopped what he was saying when his gaze snagged on a couple of guys who had entered the bar. No one had come in for a while, so it got his attention.

Cord followed his gaze. "Fuck. I hope they're boys," he whispered reverently.

Inwardly, Aaron was praying, too, especially as one of them was wearing a gorgeous skin-tight emerald green catsuit. Until he saw who it was. Zaire.

"Holy shit," he breathed, hoping he was wrong. If he was right, his life had become a walking disaster. Despite having had an idea Zaire was a boy, this could be the confirmation he needed that they were on the same page.

Zaire examined the whole room, seemingly taking in every person in the club, bypassing Aaron, then flicking back, eyes wide.

Aaron raised his eyebrows and cocked his head. "Excuse me a moment."

"Don't tell me you're…"

He didn't hear anymore because he'd walked over to Zaire. "Fancy seeing you here." He watched Zaire swallow and lick his lips.

"Same could be said for you. I would've said you were stalking me had you not been in here first." He gave a small smile, fidgeting with the belt hooks on his suit.

"You look amazing." Aaron wasn't going to deny the fact.

Crimson highlighted Zaire's cheekbones. "Thank you."

"Am I right in thinking you're a boy? And you're looking for a Daddy?" Aaron needed to know before he got his hopes up, even though he told himself to keep his hands off.

Zaire nodded, and when Aaron raised his eyebrows at him, cleared his throat and said, "Yes, I am. To both."

The tension rose between them as they stayed silent with locked gazes until Zaire blinked away.

"Well, you have plenty of Daddies to choose from. Don't be overwhelmed. Some of us have been waiting a long time to find someone."

"I didn't…You didn't…You're a Daddy?" Zaire couldn't seem to figure out what he wanted to say.

Aaron nodded. "I am. Have been for many years." He paused. "Can I buy you a drink to settle you before your first Daddy comes to visit?"

"What do you mean?" Zaire's brows snapped together.

"I can guarantee as soon as you sit down and I leave your side, you will have several Daddies come and speak to you and your friend and give you their spiel about what they can offer you. I thought you might like a drink before it happens. I don't want you to feel inundated."

Zaire glanced around and nodded. Although Zaire had appeared to be confident the previous times Aaron had seen him, he appeared nervous enough that Aaron's Daddy instincts were kicking in, and he wanted to care for his boy—a boy. Aaron cupped Zaire's elbow and guided him and his friend to the bar, allowing them both to sit while he stood in the middle of them.

"This is Colin." Zaire introduced his friend. "Colin, this is Aaron."

Colin's eyes widened as they flicked back and forth between Aaron and Zaire. It seemed Zaire had been talking about him, but what had he said?

"Nice to meet you, sir."

"You, too, Colin. Now, what would you both like to drink?"

Three beers were ordered, and once they'd arrived, Aaron said, "I mustn't keep you from finding what you came here to find. I'm over at that table," he indicated where Cord was sat, "if you need anything. Please don't think you have no one to help you should you need it. It goes for both of you. Okay?"

Both boys nodded and verbalised their understanding when Aaron indicated he wanted an answer.

He turned to leave when Zaire's voice called him back.

"Could you…" Zaire swallowed and ducked his head. "Never mind."

Aaron returned to him, lifting his chin with his forefinger. "Finish your question, please."

Zaire's gaze locked with his again, and something

charged between them. Aaron wanted to kiss him but refused to do so without giving Zaire the choice of Daddies, as much as it killed him to do so. He would've loved to offer to be Zaire's Daddy, but he was obviously a glutton for punishment because he wanted Zaire to choose him.

"Could you stay until we leave?" he whispered.

"I can and will."

Dropping his fingers from Zaire's skin, he nodded at Colin and returned to Cord.

"I see you know one of them. Why not claim him?" Cord leaned his elbows on the table, coming closer.

"It's a little complicated how I know him. As for claiming him, you should know better. They claim us, not the other way around."

Cord laughed and nodded. "They do."

"I will hang around until they leave. A friendly face and all."

"Yeah." Cord smirked. "A friendly face, okay." Disbelief rang true through his words, but Aaron ignored the implied meaning.

His gaze was on Zaire and the three men surrounding the two boys. Luckily for the men, they kept a respectful distance, and Aaron was not concerned about them pushing too hard. He'd keep an eye on them, even if it killed him.

As much as what he'd said to Cord was true, he also hated the idea Zaire might choose someone else. He wanted Zaire, and he wanted Zaire to want him back.

CHAPTER FIVE

ZAIRE

Zaire lost track of how many Daddies had come up to speak to them, but none had given him butterflies in his stomach as Aaron did. He'd been polite, yet honest with each and every one of them. In between visits, he and Colin had spoken about who they liked and who didn't match up with them. Colin had already decided who he wanted, but he refused to leave Zaire until Zaire had made his decision.

He had to get the courage up to ask the one person he wanted. His gaze flicked in Aaron's direction as it had done many times throughout the evening. Once again, he found Aaron's gaze on him, which should be unsettling, but Zaire found it reassuring.

"Why don't you go and speak to him again," Colin murmured, leaning in. "You mentioned him loads before we even arrived here, and that was when you didn't know he was a Daddy."

Knowing Colin was right, Zaire gathered his confidence, which he usually had in spades, and straightened his spine. "Okay. This is fucking scary. I thought I had enough confidence to do this with my eyes closed but the minute it became possible, I'm like a mouse."

"I know, Zaire. I'll be forever glad of your Daddy there helping us out when we first got here."

Zaire didn't reject the ownership comment, wishing it were true. "Do you want to come over with me so your new Daddy, when you tell him, can get Aaron's approval?"

Colin tilted his head. "Hmm. Yes, actually. I think it would be a good idea." Colin stood, indicating with his head to Zaire. "Come on."

Not at all prepared for the conversation he was about to have with Aaron, Zaire left his seat and followed Colin to the men's table.

"Everything okay, boys?" said a voice Zaire didn't recognise.

"We've decided, but we would like some support when we tell them if you wouldn't mind, Sirs?" Colin's respectful attitude was the perfect one for a boy, and Zaire could see why Daddies fell over themselves for him.

"Of course. Why don't you both have a seat and let us know who you've chosen?" Aaron was the one who answered that time.

"Thank you, Sirs." Colin moved to sit next to the other guy, leaving the space next to Aaron for Zaire.

Inhaling deeply, Zaire sat, his thigh touching Aaron's in the small booth.

"So, who have you chosen?" the other guy asked.

Zaire looked to Colin, begging with his eyes for Colin to go first.

"I'd like to speak some more with Dave. The guy over there with the bushy beard and grey waistcoat," Colin said in a small voice.

A whistle pierced the air as the guy next to Colin shouted over to Dave and indicated for him to come over.

Colin's face grew warm the closer Dave got to the table.

"Hey, Cord. What's up?"

"Hey, Dave. Colin here would like to speak to you more about him being your boy if you would?"

Dave's face lit up in a beaming smile. "Of course! Do you want to sit here, or shall we move to another table, Colin?"

"Um…another table is fine. I don't want to interrupt Cord and Aaron's evening any more than I have already done."

"You're not interrupting, Colin. I'll be here until you are comfortable. Okay?" Aaron said, gaze locked on Colin's.

"Yes, sir. Thank you."

When Colin smiled at Zaire as he stood and left, Zaire swallowed hard, knowing his turn was next but scared about what was to come from his revelation.

"So, Zaire," said Cord, leaning forward with a smile. "Who can we bring to the table for you?"

Zaire cleared his throat, his stare focused on his interlocked fingers on the table. "No one."

"No one? There's no one you're interested in?" Cord asked.

Zaire shook his head. "No one you need to bring to the table." He inhaled shakily and glanced to the side, locking gazes with Aaron. "He's already here."

"Fuck me," Cord muttered. "I'm going to the bar, Aaron. Have fun."

Zaire was aware of Cord leaving the table, but his focus was on Aaron, who had not stopped staring at him.

"This complicates matters," Aaron stated.

"In what way?"

"Well, there's no legal reason why a headteacher can't date a member of staff, but by offering you the position, I can be accused of favouritism."

"I won't take the job."

Aaron's eyebrows rose. "You'd give up the job for a relationship?"

"In a heartbeat." Zaire was never more certain of anything in his life.

"It's hardly fair to you."

"A good relationship is harder to find than a job." Zaire chuckled.

Aaron studied him, making him fidget. "Offer still stands for the job. We'll work our way through it if you decide to join the team."

"So…you want me?" Zaire asked in a small voice.

Aaron smiled and cupped Zaire's jaw, stroking his thumb back and forth over his cheek. "I do. But where is my confident boy hiding? The one who gives me flirty innuendos while at work. The one who reprimands strangers in bars." Aaron snickered. "Oh, that would be me."

Zaire laughed and ducked his head before lifting it again. Aaron's gaze flicked over Zaire's shoulder and back again. "Is Colin okay?"

Aaron grinned. "He's fine. Looks like you've both found a Daddy tonight."

"You know how I am. I try to be good, but it's so difficult," Zaire admitted.

"I'm here to help you now. What are your hard limits?"

"I don't like being watched. By other people, I mean. PDAs are fine, but anything more, I'm not comfortable with." He needed to stop rambling.

"Okay. What else?" Aaron's hand left his jaw and rested on top of Zaire's wringing hands.

"I don't like being tied up. Restrained. If someone held my wrists, it's fine but nothing…unbending."

"Did something happen to you?"

If any other person had asked, Zaire would've told them to mind their own business. Despite how little they knew each other, Zaire was already beginning to trust Aaron, so he nodded. "A previous partner tied me up and wouldn't undo them."

"Did he hurt you?"

"No, he just laughed and watched me struggle." Zaire swallowed and looked away. "I don't know how long it was until he finally undid the rope," he finished quietly.

"Okay. Thank you for trusting and telling me. Any more limits?"

Zaire thought for a moment. "Can't think of any."

"Okay, we'll see if any more crop up as we go along." When Zaire nodded, Aaron continued, "What type of boy are you?"

"A frustrated one?" Zaire cackled, stifling his laughter under his palm.

"There he is." Aaron smiled at him, his eyes sparkling. "There's the man I know and the boy I want to know."

Zaire shrugged. "I'm a usual boy, wanting someone to take care of him, someone to understand him." To love him. Zaire refused to say that out loud.

"Why do you keep the boy and the man separate?"

"People are unforgiving when it comes to this version of me." He waved his hand in front of himself. "I found it easier to be the working man and relax when I get home."

Aaron nodded. "Maybe we can work on merging the two and see if we can find a happy medium for you. What do you think?"

Studying the man before him, Zaire said, "I don't think we'll be able to, but I'm willing to give it a try."

"It's all I can ask of you."

"What do you want from me?"

"Obedience. Communication. Trust. Do you think you can do that?"

"Can I say I will try?" Zaire didn't want to set himself up to fail from the beginning. If he gave a definitive answer, he would be scared of disappointing them both.

Aaron smiled. "Yes, you can, although communication is vital. If at any point you don't like what's happening or don't understand why something is happening, you need to let me know. It's non-negotiable."

"Fair enough."

"I think you've probably had enough stress tonight, haven't you?" Aaron said, skimming his fingers along Zaire's jaw.

"I am feeling a bit overwhelmed," Zaire agreed.

"Let's get you home."

"What about Colin?" Zaire looked over his shoulder to where Colin sat with Dave.

"We'll ask him what he wants to do before we leave. If he wants to stay, I can get Cord to keep an eye on him. If he wants to leave, he can come with us." Aaron paused. "Did you drive here?"

Zaire shook his head. He hadn't thought it was a good idea to drive when he might need alcohol to settle his nerves. "No, we got a taxi."

"Good choice. I can drive you home."

Zaire slid out of the booth and stepped away so Aaron could do the same. Once Aaron had, he gazed at Zaire and linked their fingers together as if awaiting a rebuttal. When Zaire didn't pull away, the corner of Aaron's mouth lifted, and he directed Zaire to Colin's table.

"Sorry to interrupt, Dave. Colin's friend wanted to check his plans." Aaron glanced at Zaire, indicating with his head.

"Hey, Colin," Zaire said with a quiet voice and a

flick of his gaze to Dave. "I'm getting a lift home. Do you want to come, or are you happy here?"

He watched as twin red patches bloomed on Colin's cheeks as he smiled at Dave, and Zaire knew his answer. "I'm happy to stay. Dave said he would take me home or see me to a taxi when we've finished talking."

"I'll make sure he's safe," Dave agreed.

Aaron nodded and squeezed Zaire's hand.

"Alright. Call me tomorrow, Colin. Okay?" Zaire lifted his eyebrows, hoping Colin understood his meaning.

"I will."

"See you, Dave," Aaron said, clapping his shoulder. To Zaire, he said, "I need to say goodbye to Cord."

Zaire's heels clicked against the wooden floor of the club as he followed behind Aaron. He couldn't believe how much had changed since he'd walked through Infinity's doors. When he'd arrived, he'd hoped to find a Daddy, but he honestly hadn't believed he would. For it to end up being Aaron, who was potentially going to be his boss, was disconcerting.

Sneaking a glance at Aaron as he spoke to Cord, Zaire felt a warm sensation inside him. It was too early to tell if they were a perfect fit, but from what Zaire had witnessed other times, Aaron would be great. Time would tell if Zaire would fit with what Aaron needed. That was where all Zaire's other relationships had failed. They had told him he was an unmovable mountain who wouldn't learn the rules. Zaire stared at the floor, shoulders dropping at the memories from not one, but two Daddies. Maybe he wouldn't ever find someone who could deal with him. Maybe he should leave Aaron now and stop trying.

An arm slipped around his back, tugging him closer, and Zaire peeked up at Aaron.

"Stop thinking so hard. Wherever your mind just went, I don't like it," Aaron whispered in his ear.

Zaire didn't say anything, though he dropped his gaze once more.

"Cord, we're going to go. Zaire's feeling tired." Aaron clapped hands with Cord and guided Zaire to the exit.

Zaire peered over his shoulder for one final check on Colin, who sat in the same place with a huge smile on his face, his hand clasped in Dave's. Zaire smiled. He was so happy for Colin.

"He'll be fine. Cord will keep an eye on them as well."

Moving his gaze to Aaron's, Zaire gave a lopsided grin. "Thank you. It means a lot."

"You're welcome. I'll do anything to make you feel comfortable." They stopped. "This is me."

Aaron opened the car door, indicating for Zaire to get in, which he did. Aaron closed the door and jogged around the front of the car to the driver's side.

After he had given Aaron his home address and the car had pulled out into the night, Zaire watched the scenery in silence. He didn't know what to say. They probably had a huge amount to discuss, but he didn't want to. Zaire wanted their relationship—if they were to have one

—to progress as a normal one would. It was difficult for it to happen because there were so many boundaries usually involved in a Daddy and boy relationship.

What Zaire wanted was for his Daddy to take control and stop him from having to think about everything. He wanted to stop second-guessing his choice of outfit. He wanted to stop holding himself inside while he worked. However, as much as Aaron thought he could help Zaire to merge his two sides, Zaire had been doing it so long, he didn't think it could work. He agreed to try and try he would.

"You're thoughtful over there."

Zaire stared across at Aaron. "I'm letting it sink in you're a Daddy, although why I didn't figure it out before, I don't know."

Aaron snorted. "I'm not wearing a sign."

"I know, but most Daddies can't help their protective and caring side from showing in their daily lives. When I think back on the times I've seen you, it all seems glaringly obvious, but at the time…" Zaire shrugged, turning his gaze to the view once more.

"It's often difficult to separate the two, which I believe is why you struggle so much." Zaire gawked at him as he continued, "I don't separate myself. I am who I am. I'm a Daddy in nature, but I don't hide it away when I'm at work. Naturally, I'm not called Daddy, but a lot of the things involved in my job are helped by my personality." He paused and glanced over at Zaire, who was staring at him. "For you, it's a similar notion. Your caring side allows you to do the job you do, but you quietly suffer by hiding away who you are."

"And who am I?" Zaire whispered.

"A boy who has the chance to be a boy with the students he looks after. You get to play with them, help them, support them, just as you would if they were your best friends. If you allowed yourself, you could be a boy ninety per cent of the time."

Zaire snorted. "That won't happen. It's impossible."

"Nothing is impossible if you want it enough and have support," Aaron argued.

Thinking about Aaron's words kept him busy for the remainder of the journey. When he pulled up outside Zaire's house, Aaron stopped the engine and got out, walking around to Zaire's side and opening his door.

"Home sweet home." Aaron smiled, grabbing Zaire's hand and linking it through his arm.

Staring at the ground, Zaire withheld a smile. When they stood outside his door, the security light shining bright, Zaire inhaled. "Thank you for tonight."

"You're welcome. I hope, after you've thought some more, we can do it again and maybe have dinner?" Aaron rested his hands on Zaire's waist.

"I'd like that."

CHAPTER SIX

AARON

Aaron could feel Zaire's body trembling beneath his hands, whether from the cool wind or nerves, he wasn't sure. "I'll ring you tomorrow to see how you are." Regardless of their relationship's status, Aaron would need to make sure Zaire was alright with everything that had happened tonight, even if Zaire declined to go further.

"Okay. Thank you." Zaire's gaze flicked over his face.

Aaron pinched Zaire's chin between his finger and thumb and pressed a chaste kiss to Zaire's lips before pulling back. "Good night, Zaire."

Zaire didn't say anything, just stared, then leaned forward and fused their lips, wrapping his arms around Aaron's head and holding him tight.

Unprepared for the attack, Aaron fell back several steps until he regained his balance. He allowed the forcefulness of Zaire's kiss but slowly gentled it, cupping Zaire's jaw as Aaron held him close with the other hand. Lifting his head, he held firm when Zaire attempted to kiss him again. They both breathed heavily as they locked gazes.

"I can see I'm going to have my hands full with you," Aaron said with a smile, loving the idea.

Unfortunately, it appeared to be the wrong thing to say because Zaire immediately tensed up. His jaw firmed, and he pulled away.

Aaron frowned, thinking over what he said and seeing nothing wrong with his words. "Zaire?"

"I'm tired. Thank you for bringing me home." His voice was clipped, devoid of all warmth as he unlocked and opened his door.

Before Zaire stepped in, Aaron bit out, "Stop!" in a firm order. Zaire immediately halted, his back facing Aaron. "Turn around." Zaire did, gaze on the ground. "Eyes up." Zaire hesitated but obeyed. Aaron could see pain and strength in the eyes staring at him. "Communication is non-negotiable," he reminded Zaire. "I said something to upset you. I would like an explanation."

He hated he'd inadvertently hurt Zaire, but he couldn't address it until he knew the reason for it. Aaron certainly didn't have any issues with an unruly boy; in fact, he loved being the one to help the boy learn the rules.

As he waited for Zaire to answer, he studied his boy. Zaire's short black hair was perfectly styled; his usually flawless skin was hidden behind a layer of makeup, which made him ready for the catwalk; and his jewellery accentuated his bone structure. In short, he was fucking gorgeous.

"I..." Zaire huffed. "I've been told on more than one occasion I'm a handful and too disobedient for rules. It was why previous Daddies have left me." The last part was said in a whisper.

Aaron could have beat those other Daddies for doing this to Zaire. They were supposed to take care of their boy, not knock him down until he believed all the crap they fed him. He stepped forward, cupping Zaire's face in his hands again and staring into his eyes.

"They were wrong. Not only were they wrong about you, but they were wrong for you. If they couldn't handle you, you were not the right boy for them. I, on the other hand, can't wait to help you remember the rules. I can't wait to help you believe in yourself, to love yourself—to love both sides of yourself. When I said I was going to have my hands full, I said it with joy. I cannot wait."

He punctuated his words with a gentle kiss and wrapped his arms around Zaire, holding him tight and allowing his words to sink in as he rubbed a hand up and down his back. Aaron knew when the words seemed to hit home because Zaire's muscles loosened, and he gripped the back of Aaron's shirt, tucking his face into Aaron's neck.

When Zaire appeared boneless and almost unable to stand by himself, Aaron pulled back, ensuring Zaire was steady. "Get some sleep. I'll call you in the morning."

"Okay, Daddy."

It had seemed an automatic reaction.

Aaron watched as Zaire entered the house and locked the door before leaving. There was a lot to learn about the boy hiding behind those pain-filled eyes.

Aaron left the phone call until around eleven the next morning, not wanting to wake Zaire too early. It wasn't easy. He'd been up since seven and had already completed his home workout routine, cleaned the house, done the laundry and made a salad ready for lunch. He was restraining himself as much as possible, but he wanted nothing more than to call Zaire and make sure he was okay. Aaron didn't want Zaire to think too much because he was sure Zaire would talk himself out of their relationship. Aaron would back off if he did, but Aaron believed Zaire needed this as much as Aaron did.

When the clock finally ticked onto the eleven, Aaron already had his phone in hand and ringing.

"Hello?" Zaire's voice was quiet, reserved, so unlike his usual perky, charming self.

"Hey. How are you this morning?"

Zaire's sigh drifted through the phone, and Aaron's heart fell. "I'm a bit tired. I didn't sleep brilliantly."

"Why not, sweetheart?"

"Just…everything. So much to think through, so many decisions to make."

"I understand. Tell you what…get yourself dressed

in something comfortable that you can move in easily. I'm going to take you bowling."

"Bowling?" Zaire's tone explained exactly what Zaire thought.

"You don't like bowling?"

"Hmm. It's not usually my thing, but alright."

"Good. I'll be there in an hour. We can have lunch before we go."

"I haven't—"

"I'm bringing it with me. It's already prepared, although do you have any allergies I need to know about?"

"No, I'm fine with anything."

"Okay. Just get yourself ready. Leave everything else to me."

"Yes, Daddy."

"Good boy. See you shortly."

When Aaron ended the call, he blew out a breath. He needed to help Zaire, but he was struggling to figure out the best way to do it. The first thing he needed to do was to teach Zaire to have fun, to relax, to forget about problems for a short time because it would make it easier to deal with them.

Glad he'd already prepared a salad, Aaron quickly sliced the eggs, chopped the ham and added them and the couscous to the bowl. He packed it up with a jar of coffee in case Zaire didn't have any and headed out.

When Zaire opened his door, Aaron raised his eyebrows at his choice of clothing. Zaire's interpretation of something comfortable was black jeans and a red v-neck jumper, which, although looked fantastic on him, lacked his usual extravagance.

"You look good. Wouldn't you prefer to wear something more your style?" Aaron asked as he followed Zaire down the hall to the kitchen.

"Nah, I'm good."

Aaron pursed his lips but let the subject drop, knowing, by the sound of Zaire's voice, he shouldn't push.

The containers were placed on the counter, and Aaron divided the food between two plates, placing both on the kitchen island table along with cutlery. "Do you eat in here or somewhere else?"

Zaire shrugged. "Usually in here or on the sofa. The dining table hardly ever gets used unless people are visiting."

"Alright, here it is."

Aaron perched himself on the seat adjacent to where Zaire was, so their legs could touch if either wanted a source of comfort. To be honest, Aaron wanted to know whether Zaire would take the opportunity if it arose. Time would tell.

Throughout lunch, Aaron peppered Zaire with questions about music and films, which Zaire answered happily as he ate the lunch Aaron had prepared. Seeing it disappear made Aaron extremely satisfied.

Once they'd finished, Aaron washed up what had been used and led Zaire to his car. He opened the passenger door for him and, once he was seated, reached across to click the belt into place before closing his door. Whenever anybody asked about his need to take care of someone, he found it difficult to explain why he needed it so much. It was as if it was in his DNA.

Once they'd arrived, traded their shoes and started their game, Zaire appeared to relax, smiling more, laughing and generally having a good time, so it seemed. Aaron breathed easier knowing he had brought that joy to Zaire, despite Zaire's reluctance to begin with.

They quickly worked their way through two games, which they each won one of, before Aaron took their shoes to trade back before linking their fingers and heading for the food area.

"Would you like a cheeseburger and chips?" Aaron asked

"That would be great."

Aaron ordered two lots of the meal with drinks, paid and carried the tray to one of the high seated tables, where they could see a view of the rest of the bowling alley and people watch.

"I love watching how people act around each other. You can usually tell who has a crush on who, which couples are fighting, and who have recently started seeing each other. Have you ever people watched?"

Zaire shook his head, looking around at the customers. "No. I'm usually too preoccupied."

"Is that what happens when you're not enjoying yourself somewhere, or does it happen all the time?" Aaron asked as he dipped his chips into ketchup.

The chips were poured into the open burger container and the burger in his hands before Zaire answered, "A bit of both, I guess. I struggle to relax when I'm out unless it's somewhere I feel safe, like Infinity. Anywhere else…" He shrugged and took a bite of his burger.

"Hence this afternoon's clothing choice?" Aaron prodded.

Zaire sat back, his brow puckered as he finished what was in his mouth. "Why do you have a problem with how I'm dressed?"

"I don't have a problem with it," Aaron calmly stated. "I know it's not who you are."

"But it is! This is part of me! This is the part of me who can go out on 'normal,'" Zaire used his fingers as quotes, "dates. This is the part who won't get harassed."

"I understand. I'd love for you to be able to feel comfortable in whatever you want to wear, regardless of what other people think or say. I'd love to be your buffer, your sounding board, your reassurance, your caring, everything you need to be yourself."

"How can you? You're not with me all the time." Zaire crossed his arms on the table, gazing at his food.

"I want to give you the tools to be who you are. My support, visible when I'm with you and within your mind when I'm not, will always be there. If you can see a way of being the person you want to be all the time, I will do my best to get you to that point, and I am determined to get you there. I want you happy and whole."

Aaron's heart ached at the expression on Zaire's face. It would take a while for him to believe Aaron could do that for him. Although Aaron needed Zaire's complete trust for it to happen, which he reminded him.

"I'm working on it," Zaire said, his mouth twitching.

Aaron let the subject go, determined to bring it up another time. "What do you like to do when you're not working or at Infinity?" Seeing Zaire had finished his chips, Aaron passed a few from his plate to Zaire's, earning a smile.

"I love rock climbing."

"Rock climbing? Where do you do it? Don't you need cliffs and mountains for that?" Aaron drank some of his coffee.

Zaire chuckled, and Aaron beamed at the lightness now overtaking his features. "No. I do indoor rock climbing. There's a place on the outskirts of Cambridge which has a huge space full of different sized walls and obstacles for people to try. I've been doing it for several years now."

"You must have good upper body strength."

"Yeah. It is quite intense on the upper body, but your feet support you as well."

"Do you enter any competitions or anything?"

"No, not at the moment. I like doing it to relax. When I have to think about where my hands and feet are going, everything else recedes to the back of my mind. It's how I envisage a Daddy and boy relationship."

"Care to explain?"

Zaire picked up a chip and swirled it around in the

sauce but didn't eat it. "The Daddy looks after the boy, doing things for him and giving him time to blank his mind, not worry about everything all the time. I'd love to have that."

"And I'd love to give it to you. You need to learn to trust me. I know what I'm doing, even when it seems like I don't. I want you content, happy and safe." Aaron offered the best reassurance he could, but ultimately, it would be up to Zaire if they continued. "Come on. Let's head back."

They stood in the same places as they had done the evening prior, and Aaron was ready to leave Zaire to think when Zaire opened the house to him. "Come on in."

Aaron didn't hesitate, understanding this was something Zaire needed. He had no plans of taking things to a sexual level, but Aaron was eager to shower Zaire with whatever he would allow.

Zaire was such an enigma, and Aaron wanted to find out every little thing about him. He had his work persona, which seemed to bleed into dates when there were at places deemed unsafe. He had his boy persona, which was louder, and yet, quieter at the same time. It was almost as if Zaire himself didn't know who he wanted to be—or who he was. Aaron would love nothing more than to be the one to help him figure it out.

Even for him, a seasoned Daddy, he was struggling to discern the best way to do it. He needed to speak to Nora. Although she didn't have a boy, she had a pup;

there were similarities, and maybe she could see something Aaron had missed.

As he studied the living room, he tried to piece together a bit more information. The room was a neutral colour but had splashes of colour on the walls and fabrics throughout the space—a bit of Zaire thrown out for all to see. The sofas were large and, if Aaron wasn't mistaken, the type which would envelop a person when they sat down and have them wanting to never get back out. Aaron walked to the pictures he could see on the walls, noting Zaire as a young boy with who, he assumed, was family and pictures of various people at different ages. They told a story of a happy childhood, and Aaron sincerely hoped it had been.

"Are these your family?"

"Yes."

"You seem close."

"We were."

Aaron gritted his teeth against the need to reprimand Zaire for the lack of communication. It wasn't the right time for it, although he couldn't refrain from glancing over his shoulder at Zaire with a raised eyebrow and receiving a blush and the ducking of his head.

"Why? Are you not as close now?"

Silence greeted his answer, and when he turned, he saw Zaire clench his jaw and flare his nostrils. This would not be good.

CHAPTER SEVEN

ZAIRE

Zaire leaned back in the comfortable sofa, crossing his legs and arms as he plucked up the courage to answer Aaron's question. It wasn't that he was nervous about admitting his past; it would prove what Zaire had been saying all along: he needed to hide away certain parts of himself depending on the situation.

"I have a brother and a sister. We were close when we were younger, always in each other's pockets, especially as we are so close in age, too. Only four years separate us all." He inhaled. "When I came out to our parents, they were amazing about it. Everything a gay man could wish for." Zaire smiled in remembrance. "Zena used to caw about having a gay brother, and Zacary said it didn't change anything."

"Zaire, Zacary and Zena?" Aaron smiled.

Zaire chuckled. "Yes. I'm glad my parents stopped at three kids. Who knows what names they would've come up with?" They chuckled, then Zaire sobered, continuing with his story, "When my love of clothing and makeup began to show, my father took it badly. He stopped talking to me completely. Anything that needed to be said was passed through the other people in the family. He refused to eat at the same table as me."

Aaron came to sit next to him, resting one knee on the sofa, the other braced on the floor as his hand squeezed Zaire's knee.

"There were so many arguments between Mum and Dad," he continued quietly, his mind rolling the films of the past. "So many nights I went to bed crying because I could hear the slurs Dad had shouted about me. So, I began to change. I would only wear the clothes when I was out of sight. I'd wear boring clothes but stop at a friend's house to change. At least, until Mum yelled at me one day for forgetting who I was, for not being true to myself. It was at that point she must have reached her limit." Zaire pulled his legs up to his chest, wrapping his arms around his knees.

"What happened?"

"She kicked Dad out, telling him if he couldn't accept who his son was, he shouldn't be a father," he whispered. "I tried to be the person who they both wanted me to be."

Aaron slid his hand around Zaire's shoulders, pulling him into his body.

Voice hoarse, he forced himself to finish, "Ze blamed me for breaking up our parents' marriage, and thus the second bout of silent treatment began. Car and Mum sided with me, but Dad and Zena…" Zaire shrugged. "I see Mum all the time. Car, I don't see as much because he works abroad, but we're always on the phone."

"Car?"

Zaire chuckled, his spirits lifting a bit. "He hated our names were similar, so he started going by Car instead of Zacary."

They were silent as Aaron held Zaire tight, his cheek rubbing against the top of Zaire's head.

"I need a drink," Zaire said suddenly, sitting up out of Aaron's embrace, feeling the loss immediately. He strode to the kitchen, ready to find a beer.

"Sit down. Let me make us something," Aaron said, guiding Zaire to the chair he'd occupied earlier that day. "You've been on your feet for a while. Tell me where everything is to make hot chocolate."

"I had been thinking of something stronger," Zaire said.

"I know, but you don't need it. You need something warm."

Nodding slowly, Zaire watched as Aaron pottered around the kitchen as if he lived there. It was a fantastic feeling, and he felt his muscles begin to unwind. He rested his head on his fist and studied the sinewy muscles and strips of skin that were exposed as Aaron moved. There were never any hesitant movements, all certain and steady, going a long way to helping Zaire believe Aaron knew what he needed.

Of course, he did. He was a Daddy. He was Zaire's Daddy, and Zaire needed to start believing in him.

Aaron brought the steaming, calorie-filled drinks over to the table and, with a flourish, placed a marshmallow mountain in front of Zaire. Zaire grinned at the display and, after Aaron produced a spoon, dipped right in to taste the gooey mess.

When he'd finished with the spoon, he cupped one hand around the mug, closing his eyes at the warmth soaking into his palm and held his other hand out to Aaron, who quickly threaded their fingers together, rubbing his thumb up and down his skin.

"Your mother was right," Aaron began softly. "You don't need to be anyone but yourself. Even more so when it's just me around. I'd love to see what you're capable of when you allow yourself to be true to your inner self."

Zaire said nothing but thought hard about Aaron's words. He'd been dividing himself for so long now, he wasn't sure if he could stop. He didn't know how.

"Do you have a TV in your bedroom?" Aaron asked, disrupting his thoughts.

Zaire nodded. "Yes."

"Okay. Now we've finished our drinks, let's get you ready for bed. I can see you're tired. We can watch a film before you sleep." Aaron picked up their mugs and set about washing and drying them and the other items he'd used, then held out a hand to Zaire. "Show me the way?"

Zaire said nothing, wanting nothing more than to wrap himself around Aaron and gain a release his cock suddenly needed badly.

When they entered his bedroom, Aaron overtook

him and tugged him towards the en-suite, which could be seen from the bedroom door. He motioned for Zaire to sit on the closed toilet seat and opened the cupboards until he found Zaire's makeup remover and cotton wool. As Aaron wet the fabric and began wiping Zaire's forehead, Zaire swallowed hard and closed his eyes against tears. No one had ever done this for him.

Unsure of how much time had passed as Aaron removed his neutral makeup covering, Zaire remained relaxed and sleepy.

"There. All done. Let's get your jewellery off, now." Aaron, again, helped by removing the one necklace Zaire had allowed under his jumper and his wrist-watch. "Do you want a shower before you go to bed? I would normally say you should, but today it's your choice."

"I'd like to leave it for tonight if that's okay?" Zaire's voice was hesitant, not wanting to upset Aaron.

"It's okay for tonight. You've been through a lot today." Aaron led him back into his bedroom, stopping at the drawers. "Do you wear pyjamas?"

Zaire shook his head. "My boxers."

"Alright."

Aaron turned to him and slid his hands to the hem of Zaire's jumper, pulling it up over his head and drop-ping it to the floor beside them. He went to his knees. Zaire gasped at the sight of Aaron kneeling before him, and despite knowing nothing would happen tonight, Zaire's cock had other ideas. Aaron reached for the button on his jeans and undid them, tugging them down his legs. He removed Zaire's shoes, jeans and socks before standing once more.

"You're gorgeous, sweetheart. Let's get you into bed so you can relax."

Aaron wandered to the bed, lifting the cover for Zaire to climb in and tucked it back around him. He reached for the remote, which was on the bedside table, walked around to the other side of the bed and, after kicking off his shoes, sat on top of the covers with his back against the headboard.

Zaire had no interest in watching anything, but his gaze remained on the film, though he had no idea what it was. He was focused on being so close to Aaron in his bedroom—in his bed—and not having the energy or inclination to do anything about it.

Laid as he was, with his head on his pillow facing Aaron, he could see whenever Aaron shifted position, and he found it reassuring. Aaron's hand came to Zaire's hair and stroked the tips of his fingers through the strands, encouraging Zaire to close his eyes.

"I'm going to let you get some sleep, sweetheart," Aaron whispered from above him.

"Please?"

"What do you want, Zaire?"

"Stay until I fall asleep?" he mumbled, already halfway there.

The hand resumed its movements, and Zaire drifted off.

◄—————————►

Zaire blinked open his eyes, his eyelids repeatedly closing as he slowly roused from his sleep the following morning. As he lay there, he felt a deep boneless relaxation from which he could probably fall back to sleep again, but he wanted to bask in the feeling. Never before had anyone soothed him as he fell asleep or taken care of him as well as Aaron had the previous night. Even Zaire himself didn't take good care, though he wouldn't tell Aaron.

The covers rolled with him as he turned to his back and rubbed his eyes free of sleep. He dropped his arms heavily to the bed and stared at the ceiling, a smile curving his mouth as he remembered everything that had happened. It had been an amazing day. Even though he wasn't a fan of bowling, he'd had fun, and maybe he could persuade Aaron to try rock climbing next time.

A knock at the door had him frowning. Preparing to ignore it, he grumbled when it sounded again, so he got out of bed, pulled on some joggers and stumbled down the stairs. Seeing his reflection in the mirror by the front door had him rolling his eyes: his hair was stuck up all over the place, and he had creases on the side of his face from the pillows. Whoever was at the door would have to put up with how he looked because he didn't care.

Another knock had Zaire flinging the door open ready to curse the visitor for being impatient, but the words died on his tongue when a gorgeous headteacher smiled at him and held out a bakery carrier bag.

"Peace offering."

Zaire frowned. "Why do you need a peace offering?"

"In case I woke you up." Aaron grinned at him, and Zaire practically melted at the sight.

Aaron entered, kissing Zaire on the creased cheek and continued through to the kitchen. When Zaire followed, yawning, Aaron passed him a takeaway cup and said, "Why don't you head up for a shower and put something comfortable on. I'll make you some breakfast for when you're finished."

Zaire stared at him for a moment, saying nothing, then he put his cup on the table and walked over to Aaron. "Please, Daddy. Could I have a hug?"

Aaron's face softened, and he graced Zaire with a smile. "Of course, you can." Aaron wrapped his arms around Zaire's back and held him close, rubbing his hand up and down his back and resting his cheek against Zaire's head. Zaire turned his face into Aaron's neck and inhaled, closing his arms around Aaron's waist. Every muscle that had tensed when he'd risen from bed loosened once more, and he returned to his blissful state. What was it about Aaron that was so peaceful?

"Are you okay, Zaire?"

Zaire nodded into his shoulder, holding tighter for a moment before letting go. "Thank you for yesterday. And today."

"You don't need to thank me. I will be taking care of you a lot more now. It will give you a chance to breathe." Aaron pecked a kiss on his lips.

"Will you…" Zaire stopped, not sure if he should

be asking for this so soon into their relationship. "Never mind."

"No. It sounds important. Will I what?" Aaron gripped his hands loosely, rubbing his thumb across the back in a soothing gesture.

Zaire ducked his head, second-guessing his words but knowing Aaron wouldn't let it go. Why Zaire was so subdued and quiet when Aaron was around, Zaire had no idea. The thought had him straightening his posture and looking Aaron in the eye. "Will you help me? Shower, I mean."

For a moment, there was no change of expression on Aaron's face as his eyes roamed Zaire's features until the corner of his mouth lifted. "I'd love to."

Zaire rolled his lips inwards, trying to hide the joy he felt at being granted this wish, but he didn't think he was successful.

"Let's take our drinks with us so they don't get cold. We can drink them before we get in."

"Yes, Daddy," Zaire whispered.

Aaron threaded their fingers together and led the way up the stairs, their other hands gripping their coffees.

Zaire had showered with other Daddies, but he wasn't sure what to expect with Aaron, so he was hesitant in his movements. Aaron switched on the shower and pulled the curtain around to stop the spray from hitting the floor, laying the bathmat on the floor after.

"Rest your coffee on the windowsill for a moment." Zaire did and rested back against the sink as Aaron cupped his cheek. "I've got you, Zaire. I've got you."

Tears pricked at the corners of his eyes, and he closed them as Aaron's hands touched the waistband of his trousers, pulling it away from his body and down his legs. His cock, up to now having been soft, went half-hard in seconds as he stepped out of the joggers. Crouched in front of Zaire as he was, Aaron would not be oblivious to his state of arousal. The smirk on his face as he glanced up confirmed it. His hands returned to Zaire's waist, this time sliding his fingers between the boxers and Zaire's skin. Goosebumps rose along his body as Aaron slid the boxers over his now-hard cock and down his legs.

Zaire's hands gripped the edge of the sink behind him, and he gritted his teeth against the need to thrust into the air. How he could be so aroused so quickly, he didn't know.

Aaron stood once more, avoiding touching any part of Zaire as he did. "Drink your coffee." He pressed the cup into Zaire's hand after removing its grip from the sink.

Zaire had no idea what the coffee tasted like because his focus was on the handsome specimen undressing in front of him. Aaron's movements were not a striptease, but his gaze locked with Zaire's until he was as naked as Zaire was. He was fucking gorgeous.

Aaron picked up his cup, breaking eye contact as he drank. When he finished, he placed both their cups on the windowsill and tugged Zaire into the shower, placing him with his back against the spray and facing Aaron. Aaron took Zaire's lips in a heated kiss, his hands in Zaire's hair. It was only when they broke away for air that Zaire realised Aaron had been wetting his hair, ready for the shampoo he had squirted into his hand.

"Step forward a little," Aaron muttered. As Zaire did, Aaron massaged the gel into Zaire's hair, and Zaire's eyes closed in contentment. He repeated the action twice and walked Zaire back under the spray to rinse for the last time. He reached for the body wash.

Zaire was already rock hard. He wasn't sure he could cope with Aarons' hands on his body, but Aaron continued when no protest came from Zaire. Aaron avoided his groin area, washing everywhere else before he lathered up his hands and wrapped his hand around Zaire's cock. Zaire bit back a curse at how sensitive he was and tried to concentrate on not coming.

"Good boy. Let's get you clean, and we can have a nice relaxing day," Aaron murmured as he washed every inch of Zaire's private areas. Once he was content, Aaron guided him back under the spray and washed it all off.

Zaire didn't want to have a relaxing day. He wanted Aaron.

CHAPTER EIGHT

AARON

He probably had been a bit of a tease in the shower because he'd spent more time than was necessary on cleaning Zaire's cock and ass, but Zaire looked so blissed out as he'd done it, he couldn't resist. It was coming back to bite him now. As he dried Zaire off, flames were shooting out of his eyes, his cock an angry purple colour. But it was as good a time as any for Zaire to learn Aaron knew what was best for him, and at the moment, their relationship was new. He didn't want to fall into bed with Zaire and potentially ruin everything, even if it did sound old-fashioned.

"Daddy! Please?" Zaire asked again, his hand hovering close to his cock as if he was going to stroke it.

Aaron gripped his wrist. "Later. Maybe. You need to relax today."

"I will relax once I've had an orgasm!" Zaire yelled.

Aaron stood still, eyebrows rising at the volume of Zaire's words. There was no time like the present to begin punishment, but what to choose? He would not let Zaire come, for certain, but maybe some kneeling practice.

He pointed a finger towards the bedroom. "Wait by the bed. Now!" His voice was stern, a tone he used on pupils who needed a stricter talking to.

Zaire's eyes widened, and he swallowed as he shuffled past Aaron and out of the bathroom. Aaron took his time drying himself off and redressing. He'd already had a shower that morning, so he wasn't uncomfortable with wearing the same clothes.

When he entered the bedroom, Zaire stood with his back to Aaron, facing the bed, head lowered. Aaron sat on the edge of the bed, where Zaire could see him.

"I will not have you raise your voice to me. You may not believe I know what's best for you, but I do. I'm your Daddy." He let those words sink in and added, "Kneel."

Zaire's gaze flicked to his and down again before he dropped to the floor.

"We haven't talked about safe words. Do you have any you use other than colours?"

"No, Daddy."

"Okay. We'll use colours. Red for stop, yellow for slow down. Understood?"

"Yes, Daddy," Zaire whispered.

"You will stay kneeling, eyes lowered until your time is up. Let's see how you do with fifteen minutes."

Aaron stayed with Zaire the entire time, not wanting him to be completely alone with this first infraction. He kept silent until the time had passed, and he could kneel with Zaire and pull him off his knees and into his arms. Tears seeped into his shirt as Aaron rubbed Zaire's back and cooed in his ear.

"You're such a good boy, Zaire. My good boy. You took your punishment so well, sweetheart. Well done. Such a good boy. So good for your Daddy."

Aaron had no idea how long they stayed that way, but when he felt Zaire move, he allowed him to retreat.

"I'm sorry, Daddy. I do know you know best. I'm not used to needing to withhold orgasms. My previous Daddies didn't do that. I didn't know…" Zaire trailed off and tucked his head in Aaron's neck once more.

"I understand, Zaire. I'm here to take some of the burdens now. Try to remember to let me help."

"Yes, Daddy."

"Right. Let's go get some breakfast. Alright?"

"Okay."

He'd felt something settle further inside him when he'd had Zaire in his arms. Something felt so right about this whole situation. He wouldn't let Zaire push him away without a fight.

"Let's get you dressed."

Aaron strode to the drawers, opening the top one to find an assortment of lingerie. He looked through them until he found a lilac high waisted male thong. He closed the drawer, checking in the next, finding pyjama bottoms and chose a black silk version with a tie-pull. Not finding any tops in the drawers, he drifted over to the wardrobe, noting how quiet Zaire was.

"Bingo," he whispered as he found some thin-strapped vests. He chose a dark purple and closed the doors. He'd return for a jumper if Zaire wanted one. "Right, let's get you up." He laid the clothes on the bed next to Zaire and grabbed his hands to help him stand, which he did with a wince.

Aaron picked up the underwear and crouched down, holding them for Zaire to step into. He didn't say anything about his choice of clothing, wanting to see if Zaire refused them. Carefully, he pulled them over Zaire's ass cheeks and settled the thong in his crack, smoothing his hand over the lace as he adjusted Zaire's semi-hard cock in the front of them. He picked up the vest, helping Zaire into the fabric and settling it over his slim frame. Seeing him in those two items increased Aaron's pulse, and he looked away to regain control.

The trousers were simple to put on, and soon Zaire was covered up, though his cock was semi-hard. Aaron finally glanced at Zaire's face, expecting to find him looking uncomfortable, but to his surprise, Zaire's eyes burned with banked arousal, but the rest of him was a model of relaxed.

Which was what Aaron had been aiming for.

"Let's get breakfast." Aaron strode into the bathroom, returning with their half-full coffee cups, and balancing them in the crook of his arm, he grabbed

Zaire's hand with his free hand and led the way downstairs.

Zaire hadn't said anything, but when he'd made breakfast, Aaron would make sure Zaire was alright with what had happened.

As they sat at the table with their sausage sandwiches, Aaron checked in with Zaire, "Are you okay?"

Zaire nodded and, when he'd finished his mouthful, answered, "Yes. I feel calmer than I did before."

"Good. Are any punishments a hard limit for you?"

"None that I'm aware of, apart from what we've discussed already," Zaire replied.

"If at any time you're not happy with something, you need to let me know immediately. I will be upset if I find out you're hiding something."

"Okay."

They moved into the living room, Aaron sat at one end, reading on a book, and Zaire laid on his side with his head on Aaron's lap, tucked under a blanket while he watched You've Been Framed. Aaron hadn't asked what Zaire wanted to watch but thought something easy on the brain would be the best option, and the comedic value of watching people's mishaps was that. If Zaire did have questions, he'd be able to mull them over as he watched or enjoy the show. Which he was if his giggling was anything to go by.

Several times, Aaron found himself watching Zaire's partial expression as he chuckled at the crazy antics. He wondered how often Zaire allowed himself this time to relax fully, and if he was a betting man, it wouldn't be often, if at all.

When Zaire yawned, Aaron decided to get them moving so Zaire didn't ruin his sleep pattern as he had to work the next day. "Hey, sweetheart." He waited until Zaire rolled his head to meet his gaze. "Shall we go for a run?" He smiled when Zaire's eyes lit up.

"Yes, please, Daddy!" Zaire flicked the blanket off and scrambled up, getting tangled in the process.

"Slow down, Zaire!" Aaron laughed as he helped pull the blanket from around his feet. "You'll have an accident, and we won't be able to go anywhere but the hospital." Obviously, Zaire either didn't feel any ache in his knees or didn't care.

"Sorry."

"It's okay. Just be careful, sweetheart." Aaron stood and held out his hand. "Let's find you something to wear."

After entering Zaire's bedroom, Aaron dropped Zaire's hand and strode to the drawers. When he'd chosen boxers, joggers and socks, he grabbed a t-shirt from the wardrobe and went to stand in front of Zaire. He dropped the clothes on the bed and instructed Zaire to lift his arms. As he slid the material over his head, Aaron gritted his teeth against the need to kiss the expanse of skin revealed. Laying the vest on the bed, he picked up the t-shirt and helped Zaire to put it on.

He kneeled. His hands went to the pull cord of the pyjama bottoms and pulled it free, allowing the material to puddle around Zaire's ankles. Aaron glanced up at him, watching as twin red spots bloomed on Zaire's cheeks. Only the knowledge of where they were going enabled Aaron to strip off Zaire's lacy underwear and replace them with boxers, which would be more comfortable when running. It had been warm when he'd arrived at Zaire's that morning, and although it had been several hours, it should be nice enough to run without an outer layer.

"Come on." Aaron stopped by the kitchen to grab two bottles of water and, passing one to Zaire, indicated the door. "Shall we take a jog along the river?"

Zaire's eyes lit up again, and Aaron decided there and then he would do everything in his power to make sure Zaire had that expression as often as possible.

Jogging along the River Cam had been enlightening. Aaron had been there many times before but seeing it through Zaire's eyes as he exclaimed at the canoes, rowing boats, ducks, swans and everything else he saw was...educational. It showed Zaire's love of water, which Aaron neatly tucked away for future reference.

After they'd returned, they showered together again, this time quicker and less handsy, but no less clean. Aaron had dressed himself in the clothes he'd had in his car and helped Zaire back into what Aaron had dressed him in after their first shower.

They ordered an Indian takeaway for dinner and argued the merits of several aspects of the school system. It reminded Aaron he'd done none of the work he'd brought home from school over the weekend. Luckily, it wasn't essential. Aaron had only taken it because he'd expected to be alone. He was more than happy with his surprise alternate plans.

A full stomach seemed to sap all of Zaire's energy, or maybe it was the busy day he'd had, but Aaron tugged him up the stairs once more. Zaire groaned as they climbed, grabbing hold of Aaron's hand with both of his and leaning most of his weight on him, so Aaron was literally dragging him up. When they reached the top, Aaron wrapped his arm around Zaire, laughing.

"Did you enjoy that?" he asked, kissing the side of Zaire's head.

"You made me walk up the stairs after eating, so it's your fault," he pouted, lips pursed.

Aaron caught them in a kiss as they stumbled through the bedroom door. Keeping his eyes open, Aaron directed Zaire to the bed, his hands busy roaming across Zaire's satin clad body until they cupped his ass gently.

Breaking away to breathe, Aaron slid his hands upwards, underneath the satin vest top and along Zaire's spine. "You've been such a good boy for me today, Zaire. I think you deserve a treat."

"But I wasn't a good boy this morning. I yelled at you." Zaire's voice was low and tinged with sadness.

"But you took your punishment, and all was forgiven, wasn't it?" Aaron reminded him.

"Yes, but—"

"You don't need to worry about what you think you

deserve, my sweet boy. It's my job now. And I say you deserve a treat."

Aaron cupped Zaire's face in his hands and reverently kissed his lips. He licked along the seam of Zaire's mouth, and Zaire dropped his head back on a moan, opening to Aaron's exploration. He felt Zaire sway until Zaire gripped the sides of Aaron's t-shirt, holding himself steady. Leaving his face, Aaron's hands slid down, undoing the cords for Zaire's trousers and allowing them to fall, leaving Zaire clad in a satin vest and lacy thong.

Lack of air had them pulling apart. "On the bed, sweetheart." He watched as Zaire glanced behind him, sat on the edge of the bed and slid himself over the covers until his head rested on a pillow.

Naughty boy that he was, Zaire proceeded to widen his legs and run his hands over his body in a teasing display. Stripping off his t-shirt and jeans, Aaron allowed the touches until he crawled onto the bed.

"Now, who said you could touch what is mine?" he growled as he caged Zaire between his arms.

Zaire froze, mouth gaping before snapping shut. "Sorry, Daddy. I...I need...I..." He panted, seemingly unable to get his thoughts in order.

Aaron inhaled deeply. If this was how Zaire acted when he'd hardly been touched, how much would he come apart when Aaron was balls deep inside him? Swallowing hard, Aaron leaned down and took Zaire's mouth in a hard kiss, demanding entry and insisting on a reaction. When his arms began to shake with the intensity of the kiss, Aaron lowered to his forearms, sinking his lower body onto Zaire's and groaning into each other's mouths as their dicks came into contact.

But this wasn't for Aaron. This was Zaire's treat. So, Aaron detoured from Zaire's mouth, kissing, nibbling and licking his way down the column of his neck, along his collarbones, down his sternum, shifting the vest up under Zaire's armpits as he diverted briefly to Zaire's sweet little nubs and continued down his abs, finding the barest hint of a trail heading into the lacy thong.

As he licked across the waistband of the lilac fabric, Aaron glanced up at Zaire's face, knowing he would do everything in his power to keep this man.

CHAPTER NINE

ZAIRE

He had died and gone to heaven. He must have because pleasure streamed through his whole body, tingling his extremities and leaving goosebumps along his skin. No one had ever made him feel the way Aaron did. Everything he did was to enhance Zaire's pleasure. Zaire could feel it.

As Aaron concentrated his attention on Zaire's lacy thong, Zaire gripped the sheets below him, wanting so much to touch his own body and Aaron's but knowing he hadn't been given permission. He had to endure. This was his reward, after all. Although, he couldn't understand why he was being rewarded when he'd been such a bitch earlier.

He wasn't going to complain.

As Aaron mouthed along his cock through the lace, it became even harder if it was possible, and Zaire moaned at the feel of its confinement. He needed to be free of the lace, regardless of how sexy it made him feel.

Aaron must have heard his thoughts because he lifted the front edge of the thong and allowed his cock to peek out of the top. Zaire breathed out his relief and sucked in air as Aaron's tongue lapped at the crown. He widened his legs at Aaron's insistence, rolling his head on the pillow as Aaron's hand fondled his balls, and a finger slipped under the thong, pulling it away from his crack.

A finger pressed against his hole, rubbing in circles around the muscles before pressing and retreating, never actually entering. Aaron lifted his head and swiped his finger along his own tongue. Zaire's eyebrows drew together in confusion until he saw the white fluid clinging to Aaron's finger. Aaron replaced the finger at Zaire's ass, Zaire's own precome being used as lube. It wouldn't be enough if he intended to have a cock in his ass, but a finger was fine, especially as Aaron sucked the head of his dick into his mouth, tonguing the underside as his hands continued to be busy.

Sweat was beading on Zaire's skin as he fought against his climax. He wanted to come more than ever, but his Daddy had not said he could. He wanted to be good for him, but it was becoming more difficult with each suck, with each finger press and with each tug on his balls.

"Daddy!"

Aaron lifted off his cock much to Zaire's disappointment, but it was only for four words to escape, "Come for me, sweetheart."

Zaire stared into those russet-brown eyes, twinkling in the fading light, and his body took over, clenching and releasing as he watched through half-lidded eyes as Aaron swallowed every drop. Zaire's breath was nonexistent, and his body curled in on itself.

Finally, his body slumped to the bed, and he closed his eyes.

Distantly, he heard Aaron moving around the room. He felt his thong being removed and a warm cloth sweeping over his body. He couldn't open his eyes to express his gratitude. He was exhausted.

Aaron slid his arms under Zaire's body and moved him to one side, pulling the covers over the top of him once he was free of them. Zaire wanted to speak to Aaron, but he was being pulled under by sleep.

⟵————————⟶

His alarm woke him, and Zaire flapped his hand around, trying to find his phone to turn it off. His muscles were heavy from sleep and relaxation, and he didn't want to move. But he had a job to do. Rubbing a hand over his face, he remembered the previous night and lifted his head quickly, glancing around for evidence Aaron was still there. It was a stupid thought because he knew Aaron had to work today as well, and he was sure Aaron would already be there as it was already seven on a Monday morning.

When no evidence was found, Zaire dropped his head back to the pillow and stared at the ceiling before he grinned. What a treat he'd been given. He hoped he'd be able to return the favour soon.

He swung his legs over the side of the bed, sitting upright, and spotted a piece of paper and pen on the bedside table.

Zaire,

I've locked everything up and taken the spare key with me as I didn't want to post it back through your door in case someone managed to reach through and grab it. I'll give it back to you today. I would like for you to still work at the school, but it's your choice. If you decide to accept the offer, go and see Pamela for the paperwork and make sure you attend the staff meeting straight after work today. I'd like to introduce you to everyone.

Now, be a good boy. I made you a fruit salad for breakfast, which is in the fridge, along with a packed lunch for today. I'd like you to try and eat everything, please. You need your energy.

I'm sure I'll see you at work. I'm sorry if it makes things difficult for you. Make sure you tell me if anyone gives you grief about anything. And no, I'm not only saying that to you…I say that to all my staff.

A

x

Zaire smiled at the kiss on the bottom of the note. He had been going back and forth about the position at Aaron's school, but if Aaron thought it would work, Zaire wanted to try. The job would give him a break from having to travel so far some days, he would get to know the children better than he would if he had only been there for a day or two, and he would get to work alongside some fantastic staff.

Mind made up, Zaire got ready for work.

A school day later showed Zaire he was right in choosing to work there. He'd been there for two weeks as a temp already but having agreed to a permanent position had staff coming by to see the new guy. News travelled fast.

When he finished grabbing all his things from the classroom, Zaire followed Uma to the staff room.

"We have these meetings once a week to go over different aspects of the school. Sometimes it's relevant to our class, other times it isn't, but there is always a bit of learning in there as well, so most of us try to attend regardless." Having been there for over ten years, Uma was a font of knowledge which Zaire would do well to learn from. Zaire had been in the school environment for as many years, but he didn't know the rules for this school. "Aaron has only been here a short time, but he has done so much for us already. I hope he plans on staying for the long term."

"Why would you think he wouldn't? He wasn't brought in as a temporary headteacher, was he?" Nerves roiled in Zaire's stomach at the thought Aaron wasn't staying around long term.

"Oh, no! He was brought in permanently, but you never know. Personal circumstances and all," Uma said quickly, diffusing Zaire's nerves. "Nobody knows what's going to happen in the future, do we?"

Zaire shook his head, knowing far better than she realised about the statement.

They entered the staff room, and Zaire's eyebrows rose when he saw it held a lot of people. A lot. It looked like the whole school was here, excluding temporary staff, that is, but it was a fair number of people. His gaze wandered around the people, trying to spot Aaron, whom he had not seen at all that day, but couldn't see him. He followed Uma to the far side of the room and sat down behind her as there were only a few chairs left. He could feel the heat of the sun through the windows on his back, and he closed his eyes and smiled at the warmth beginning to relax muscles he hadn't realised were tense. He had no idea how this was meeting was going to go. He only knew Aaron was planning on introducing him to the rest of the staff.

The door opened, and Pamela and another person came in, followed by Aaron with his head thrown back in laughter. Zaire's breath caught in his throat as he watched Aaron smile at the women and gesture for them to sit. Aaron's defined muscles were hidden from view under a navy-blue suit and white shirt, but Zaire knew what he looked like, and he salivated thinking about it. He couldn't keep his eyes off him, and Aaron's gaze surveyed the room, pausing with the corners of his mouth curling up when he arrived at

Zaire, then carried on. Zaire's heart raced so fast, he was sure Uma would be able to hear it. He didn't expect any acknowledgement from Aaron, apart from being a new teaching assistant but seeing the secretive smile made Zaire's day.

"Good afternoon, everyone," Aaron said, taking a seat at the front of the semi-circle of chairs. "I know you probably have questions about last week's meeting, so let's start with those."

For the next few minutes, Zaire listened as several staff members expressed their displeasure at some new procedures being put into place, but he noticed most of them were the older staff members. He surmised they were set in their ways and didn't like change, although it could be him stereotyping, and he could be completely wrong.

"Okay, so let's move on. I'd like to introduce two new members of staff: Amy and Zaire." Aaron pointed them both out, and Zaire held up his hand in greeting. "Amy will be working in Simon's class for the foreseeable future, and Zaire will be with Uma. I am in the process of sourcing one more permanent member of staff, but at the moment, I haven't found someone suitable."

Aaron spent a few minutes listening to staff who believed they needed extra staff before he continued talking. "Listening to your requests has brought me to my next announcement. My plan over the next few months is to spend a day in each class. When I'm there, I would like for you to treat me as a teaching assistant. That means you need to go about your job as you usually would and send me to do the things you need me to do." He chuckled after scanning the room. "I am not there to trip you up. I want to figure out what things would make your life easier, and I can't do that from my office."

The authority in Aaron's voice was arousing, and despite his surroundings, Zaire squirmed on his chair as his dick hardened. His gaze was riveted on the man at the front of the room. The man who took care of him and turned him on like no one had before. Zaire swore he could smell Aaron's scent from where he was, although he knew it was impossible. He swallowed hard as the gaze of the man himself locked with his for a few seconds before flitting away. Zaire inhaled slowly, jaw clenched against the need coursing through his body. He didn't think Aaron seemed as affected as he was, which was unfair. Zaire knew they weren't going to flaunt their relationship, but he could've acknowledged him in some way.

Zaire pursed his lips, withholding a smile. Maybe he could see if he affected Aaron as much as Aaron affected him. The next time Aaron's gaze slid to his, Zaire licked his lips, and Aaron's eyes widened. The next time, Zaire made a show of unbuttoning the top button of his shirt and caressing his neck. The following time, he ran his fingers along his mouth, his tongue flicking out briefly.

Aaron cleared his throat and clenched his jaw, and Zaire knew he was getting to him. He cast a glance around, seeing everyone else was facing away from him or hidden behind others, so he took a chance and slid his finger into his mouth and closed his eyes as he sucked.

"Right!" Aaron's voice boomed across the room, making Zaire jump and think he'd pushed Aaron too far. "I think that's it, so unless anyone has any questions, we'll leave it there."

Staff began mingling around, gathering their belongings as they chatted with the people close to them, the noise level steadily rising.

"Looks like you'll get to know Aaron a lot better," a voice commented, and Zaire turned to see a guy he didn't know. The guy held out his hand. "I'm Simon. I teach Year Six."

Zaire slid his hand into Simon's, panic flooding his body as he wondered what Simon had seen. "Zaire. Nice to meet you. What do you mean?"

Simon's gaze slid to Aaron, and Zaire felt his stomach pinch when he watched Simon look Aaron up and down and lick his lips. "He's visiting the classes, isn't he? So, you'll get to know him better."

Zaire didn't know Simon at all, but he had the feeling there was an underlying meaning to his words which Zaire didn't understand. Simon's gaze was on Aaron, and Zaire narrowed his eyes, wondering if there was a past relationship between the two men. It certainly seemed that way. At least from Simon's behaviour. Zaire glanced over at Aaron, seeing him in conversation with another teacher.

"Yeah, I guess. I have to head out but nice to meet you, Simon," Zaire lied through his teeth as he gathered his belongings and, saying goodbye to Uma, left the room. He didn't know why it was bothering him so much. Both had pasts they had yet to discuss in detail. Having it thrown in his face, though? It hurt as much as Zena turning her back on him, which was a shock for Zaire. Aaron could've at least warned him Zaire would probably meet someone he'd been with from the school. It might not have hurt so much. He thought he meant something to Aaron. Maybe Zaire had made a mistake taking this job.

His heart wrenched at the thought of leaving the school, especially as he had already made some friends there. It might be the best idea. He didn't think he could see Aaron every day and not remember what he thought they'd had.

He stuck his phone onto his magnetic holder in his car after dropping into the driver's seat and dialled Rod, flicking it to speakerphone. Clicking his seat belt into place, Zaire pulled out of the school car park and pointed the car towards home.

"Hey, Zaire! How's it going?"

"Yeah, good. Do you fancy going out tonight?" Zaire's tone was clipped, and he knew Rod would pick up on it.

"Sure?" Rod's voice was questioning, but Zaire couldn't talk about it without a few beers in him.

"Great. I'll be at our usual bar at…" he checked the clock, "six." His voice cracked on the last word, and he inhaled roughly, trying to keep his composure enough to get home.

"Alright. See you there."

Zaire hung up without answering, his throat thick

with unshed tears. How could the relationship be over so quickly? He'd believed Aaron was different, that Zaire meant something to him, but he supposed he shouldn't believe anyone anymore. Hadn't he learned his lesson with the last few Daddy relationships?

CHAPTER TEN

AARON

Aaron couldn't believe Zaire's audacity. With every flick of his tongue or slide of his fingers, Zaire had Aaron hardening in his trousers...trousers that would show every inch. He ended the meeting without focusing on Zaire again and got distracted by several staff members wanting to ask questions. By the time he was free, Zaire had gone, but Simon was still present. Aaron inwardly rolled his eyes. Ever since Aaron had started, Simon had been insinuating they should get together, being the only gay guys in the school. Firstly, Simon was wrong; there were at least two other people in the school, they kept themselves to themselves, unlike Simon. Secondly, Simon was not Aaron's type, and he didn't seem to get the hints Aaron kept giving him.

"Hey, Aaron."

"Good afternoon, Simon." He refused to be

brought further into a conversation unless he truly had no other option.

"So, you're going to be in my class at some point, are you?" Simon stepped close…too close for Aaron's liking.

He made a show of heading to his bag and hooking it on his shoulder. "Yes, I will be in every class over the next few months." And if Aaron had his way, Simon's would be one of the last.

"That's good to know. I'll make sure you feel welcome."

"Hopefully, you make all the staff in your class feel welcome," Aaron said, quirking an eyebrow.

"Of course!" Simon waved his hand, dismissing Aaron's concern. "The new guy seems nice."

The tone in Simon's voice caught Aaron's notice, and he shifted to face Simon, trying to show nonchalance. "Both new people are great. It's why I hired them. If there's nothing else, Simon, I have to go."

He bid goodbye. He wanted to get in contact with Zaire as soon as possible. He'd missed seeing him today. How he'd become so enamoured with the guy in such a short time, he'd never know. Grabbing his final things from his office, he exited the school and began the drive home, dialling Zaire on the journey. The phone rang but went to voicemail, so Aaron left a brief message, asking Zaire to call him when he had a minute. When he arrived home, he'd not received a call or message, so he sent Zaire a text as well.

Hi. I'm happy you decided to join the team. You'll do great. Would you like to come around for a late dinner? x

Hopefully, Zaire would get the message and accept. Aaron liked the idea of making some dinner for them both and pampering Zaire.

When he'd not received a message an hour later, Aaron tried calling again, to no avail. An hour after, he tried again. By this point, he was getting worried something had happened to Zaire. He had no other contact details for anyone in Zaire's life, so had no way of knowing if something happened to him.

He paced the living room, running his hands repeatedly through his hair and scratching his beard. When his phone rang, he dived for it, shoulders releasing when he saw it was Zaire.

"Zaire? Is everything okay?" He couldn't help the worried tone that escaped.

"Sorry, it's Rod, Zaire's friend."

"Is Zaire okay? Where is he? What's wrong?"

"Woah, slow down. Everything's fine. Or at least it would be if I didn't have a completely wasted Zaire in my company."

"He's drunk?" Aaron was surprised. Not that Zaire was drunk, but why was he drunk?

"Yep, and he needs looking after. I hear you're the person for the job." The humour in Rod's voice had Aaron relaxing.

"I am. Where are you?"

"In a taxi. The driver is patiently waiting for your address so I can bring Zaire to you."

Aaron gave Rod his address and hung up. He moved his pacing to the hallway as he waited for them to arrive. When he heard a car pull up, he threw the door open and stalked down the path. The taxi door opened, and Aaron quickly caught the body that almost fell out of the car.

"Fuh," Zaire laughed uncontrollably as he gripped Aaron's arm. "Hey, I know you." Zaire's words merged as his tongue fought to work properly.

Rod exited the taxi, asking him to wait for him to come back. "Sorry, he jumped out quicker than I could grab him."

"No problem. What caused this? I didn't think Zaire ever got like this," Aaron questioned as he helped Zaire up the path to the house.

"You caused this."

Aaron whipped his gaze to Rod's in confusion. "What do you mean I caused this? Everything has been fine between us." He continued into the house.

"Well, obviously not. You need to ask your past relationships to stop butting into your current relationships. That is if it is a past relationship."

"If what is a past relationship? You're making no sense." Aaron led an almost comatose Zaire to the sofa, laying him down and covering him with a blanket.

"According to Zaire, after he'd had a few drinks inside him, a guy cornered him at the meeting today, making insinuations. Zaire got upset you hadn't told him about your past with any staff, and it hurt him."

"You're not making sense, Rod. I've not had a relationship with anyone from scho—fuck! Simon." Aaron threaded his hands through his hair.

"He mentioned Simon, yes. You need to tell Zaire about the guy, and anyone else he might run into."

"He's got it wrong. You've got it wrong. Simon and I have never been in a relationship, never will be if I have anything to say about it. He's been flirting with me from the moment I started at the school. But I have never touched him."

"Then you need to explain to Zaire because he was completely broken up about it. Said he wasn't going to trust anyone, especially Daddies anymore. He can't go through life like that."

"I know. I will speak to him. I need to get him through tonight first." Aaron stared at Zaire. "He's going to feel like hell tomorrow." Aaron smiled. "And, although I will talk to him, he's going to hate his punishment for making me worry like that."

"It seems like he's in good hands. I better go; otherwise, I'll have to remortgage my house to pay for the taxi fare."

"Thanks, Rod, and here's my number in case you want to check up on him."

They parted ways, and Aaron locked up. Checking once more on Zaire, he pottered around, making sure he put plenty of water and painkillers in the bedroom, including two buckets—wash one, use one—some washcloths and a towel. Once he was certain he had everything he might need overnight, Aaron returned downstairs and hooked his arms under Zaire's back and knees before lifting him and carrying him to bed. There was going to be a harsh discussion and punishment the following day, but for now, he had to care for his boy. Both were going to be exhausted for school in the morning.

←——————————→

When his alarm blared through the silence, Aaron groaned and rolled over to turn it off. He'd barely had a couple of hours sleep. Zaire had been up throughout the night, alternating throwing up with sleeping, but Aaron couldn't sleep in case something happened to him. It was only when Zaire had finally seemed more settled Aaron had allowed himself to sink into the mattress next to Zaire.

Aaron's head pounded from lack of sleep, but he bet Zaire's head was worse. Glancing over his shoulder, he saw the object of his thoughts splayed out across the bed, snoring softly. A grin stole across Aaron's face, and he wished he could've taken a picture. Zaire looked so innocent. Aaron smirked when he thought about punishing Zaire that evening. It was going to be two-fold. After the display at the staff meeting, trying to get Aaron aroused while in the presence of other people, and the misunderstanding making Aaron worry something had happened to him, Zaire would have to put up with Aaron's decision on his punishment.

After setting the shower going, he returned for Zaire, picking him up and carrying his dead weight to the bathroom. Aaron had stripped him to his boxers the previous evening, so it was all he had to struggle to remove before walking into the shower, holding Zaire. Luckily, his shower was large enough for him to manoeuvre easily.

Zaire woke suddenly, clutching at Aaron's neck when the water touched his skin. "What the—"

"Shh. Calm down. Everything is okay," Aaron crooned, holding Zaire tighter, so he didn't drop him during his squirming.

Zaire stared at Aaron, his eyes widening, Aaron assumed because Zaire hadn't realised he was at Aaron's house. "What...? When...?" Zaire shook his head and winced.

"Take it easy. You'll have a sore head this morning. Slow movements are best." Aaron lowered Zaire to his feet, holding tight to his waist until he was sure Zaire was steady. "You'll regret all the alcohol today."

Zaire's cheeks flushed as he inspected the floor. "Yes, definitely regretting it," he whispered.

"Let's get you cleaned up. You'll be sweating alcohol for a while, but we can get rid of some of it." Aaron reached for the soap and lathered his hands, running them all over Zaire's body with a pretended indifference. He ignored Zaire's hard cock—morning wood was morning wood regardless of how drunk the person was the previous evening—and focused on getting him clean. After he'd finished and rinsed Zaire, he noticed Zaire was gripping the tiles and breathing heavily through his mouth. "Are you feeling okay?"

Zaire shook his head slowly, exhaling deeply. "I need…" He inhaled again. "I need to sit down."

Aaron switched off the water and opened the shower door, holding Zaire's hand as he followed. He wrapped a towel around Zaire, not bothering to dry him, and guided him back to the bedroom, where he sat Zaire on the bed. He didn't have any clothes for Zaire, and he refused to let him wear what he was wearing yesterday, so he found a pair of joggers and a t-shirt that would bury Zaire but would allow him cover as Aaron drove him home to change for work. It was the reason why Aaron had set his alarm so bloody early.

When he turned and saw Zaire studying the floor while wrapped in a large fluffy towel, Aaron thought he looked so young. There was an eight-year difference between them, but, at that moment, it felt like more.

"Zaire," he said when he stood in front of his boy. Zaire met his gaze, and Aaron's heart broke at the sorrow bleeding from them. He kneeled, resting his hands on Zaire's thighs. "I promise nothing has happened or ever will happen between Simon and me. You are the first person within the same work environment I have ever been close to. Please believe me. No matter what anyone else says, that is the truth." Aaron watched Zaire sit straighter, his lips tightening, so he continued, hoping to make Zaire understand, "Simon wants more. He has since I started working there, but I have rebuffed every comment and invitation he has offered. It's you I want, sweet boy. And I don't think you realise how much."

Tears cascaded down Zaire's cheeks, and Aaron cupped his face, reverently touching their lips together in a salty kiss.

"Ow," Zaire whispered. "Crying hurts my head."

Aaron chuckled. "I can imagine it does." He wiped away Zaire's tears. "Let's get you dressed so we can get you home."

They worked together to get Zaire into the larger clothes, laughing when they saw the result. Zaire looked like a kid playing dress-up in his parent's clothes. After a quick breakfast of toast, they drove towards Zaire's house, and Aaron dropped his bombshell.

"After work, you will return to my house. When you arrive, you will be punished for your behaviour."

He saw Zaire's head whipped in Aaron's direction from the corner of his eye, his gaze on the road ahead as it was. "What? Why do I get punished?"

Aaron quirked a brow. "Have you so conveniently forgotten your behaviour at the meeting yesterday?"

Zaire said nothing, just returned his gaze to his surroundings. Aaron thought he heard a muttered, "Shit," but he wasn't certain.

"Understand?"

"Yes," Zaire mumbled.

"Yes, what?"

Zaire sighed. "Yes, Daddy." Zaire linked his fingers in his lap, squeezing them together.

"Good boy." Aaron reached a hand over and placed it on Zaire's, rubbing his thumb against his fingers and, hopefully, soothing his worry. "Are you okay?"

Zaire moved his hand, threading their fingers together. "Yes, I'm okay. Apart from an awful headache, which is easing now the painkillers are kicking in. I expect today to be hell on earth, but I'll be fine."

"I know you will. You're strong. Just remember to drink plenty of water." Aaron had a thought. "Did you drive to the bar last night?"

"No, I drove home first and got a taxi. I knew it would be an…enthusiastic night." Zaire gave a half-smile.

Aaron squeezed his hand again and smiled at him. "I'm glad you were sensible. You make me proud, sweetheart."

"Except when I'm an asshole," Zaire muttered.

"Stop! You don't ever call yourself that." Aaron's voice rose in the small area. "You are not an asshole and never will be. Certain people, yes. You, hell no. You made a bad choice. I agree. But it does not make you an asshole."

They were quiet for a while after his outburst, and he wondered whether he'd gone too far until Zaire spoke, "Thank you for believing in me. Although I remember someone else calling me an asshole before."

Aaron chuckled. "You told me to. I will believe in you always. Even when you don't believe in yourself. Especially then."

They lapsed into silence for the remainder of the

journey. When they arrived, Aaron exited the car to help Zaire to his house but remained on the porch.

"You need to get ready, and you don't need me helping." He smirked. "We'd end up being late, and neither of us needs that."

"Okay, Daddy. Thank you for everything."

Aaron wrapped his hands around Zaire's back and kissed his forehead. "You're welcome. Remember what I said. Straight to my house after work." He pulled back and fixed a stare on Zaire until he nodded. "Good boy." He pressed another kiss to his lips and pulled away, waving over his shoulder when he reached his car.

Today was going to be a long day.

CHAPTER ELEVEN

ZAIRE

Regardless of what Aaron said, Zaire couldn't help but think of himself as an asshole. He hadn't even waited to get Aaron's side of the story from him before he thought the worst and put Aaron in the same category as the other Daddies Aaron had said treated Zaire wrongly. As he dressed for the day, he winced with every movement, his head complaining at him for his foolish antics. Rod had been a great listener, but maybe Zaire had told him too much about his relationship with Aaron. There was nothing he could do about it now, but he grabbed his phone and messaged him, apologising for being a crap friend before he hightailed it out of the door and to his car; otherwise, he would be late.

When he arrived at the school, he grabbed his bag and…shit, he'd forgotten to pack his lunch. He'd have to make do with whatever snacks he had in his bag. As he walked towards the school, he saw Aaron in his office on the telephone. He looked impeccable as always. A small smile graced his lips when he saw Aaron notice him and wave him in. Forehead creasing, Zaire headed straight towards the headteacher's office.

"Good morning, Pamela," he said.

"Morning, Zaire. Everything okay?" They fiddled with a few files on their table as they spoke.

"Yes, thanks. Aaron—Mr Brown—waved me in through the window. Not sure why."

"Okay, bear with me a sec." They scurried out of their chair, knocking quietly on the door and poked their head through. Lowered voices were heard, and they came back out, indicating for him to go in. "Yes, you're good. He's finished on the phone." They resumed their seat.

"Thanks." He headed through the open door, closing it when Aaron told him to. "Is everything okay?"

Aaron nodded with a smile. "Yeah. I have something for you." He pulled a white paper bag from under his desk and held it out. "I wasn't sure if you'd remember your lunch, so I got something for you from the deli when I got mine. If you have something, this can go in the fridge for tomorrow instead."

Zaire's throat narrowed, and he swallowed convulsively. He couldn't believe he was so lucky to have this man as his Daddy. He wanted nothing more than to go over and wrap his arms around Aaron and never let go. How he ever thought Aaron had been lying to him, he had no idea.

"Zaire?" Aaron came around the desk, and Zaire was worried he would do as he wanted, so he held out his hand palm forward. Aaron stopped, a frown on his face as he scanned Zaire from head to toe. "What's wrong?"

"I…You…God!" He rubbed a hand over his face and tried to regain his composure. After breathing deeply for a few moments, he managed to say, "Thank you so much." He waved his hand towards the bag in Aaron's hand. "For this. For everything you've given me so far. It's so much more than any other Daddy did. It seems completely unreal. I'm…" he broke off, not able to say anymore without bursting into tears.

"I understand. Take a few deep breaths, sweet boy," Aaron said in a low voice. "It can be overwhelming when you haven't had this before. If you want me to stop, I can, but I would like it if you could come to enjoy these little…gifts from me to you."

"Don't stop," he whispered.

Aaron smiled, but his mouth curled down when he looked out the window. "Take this and head to the staff toilets for a few minutes. I'll send a message to Uma that you'll be a few minutes late because I've asked you to do something. Once you feel able, head to work. Okay?" Zaire nodded. "Words, sweetheart."

"Yes…Daddy." The final word was mouthed rather than spoken.

"I really want to hug you right now, but I can't. I'm so sorry."

Zaire gazed at him, a smile gracing his face now he was settling again. The alcohol last night must have broken down some more of his walls because he wasn't usually so emotional. He took the bag Aaron passed him, grinned as best he could and sauntered out of the office to the toilets. Even being in Aaron's company had settled something inside him.

When he finally got to class, Uma sent him a worried gaze, and he knew nothing would get past her. It was a matter of time before she asked him if he was okay. Could he do this secret relationship? How was it even going to be possible?

Uma finally caught up to him at the children's break time, when one of the staff was covering while he helped Uma do some organising for the next part of the day.

"Is everything alright with you? You seem...out of sorts, today?"

Zaire laughed. "Is that your way of telling me I look like shit?"

Uma's eyes widened, then she chuckled. "No, although you do look a little worse for wear."

"Yeah, I had a long night last night. Too much alcohol was involved. I promise that is not my normal situation. I'm usually a lot more put together than this." He was worried she wouldn't want him in the class if he was deemed unreliable.

"Don't be silly. Of course, I know this isn't you. It's why I'm so worried. Is there anything I can help with?"

Zaire's heart softened. Uma was a generous and gentle soul. "No but thank you for the offer."

"Well, you know where I am if you need anything at all."

"Thank you."

The rest of the day was uneventful apart from when he opened his deli bag and saw a chicken salad sandwich, a small pot of pasta and two pieces of fruit along with an apple juice. Zaire had felt tears pricking again but refused to allow them free. Rod had replied to his message as well, telling him to stop being a jerk and talk to his Daddy. He'd rolled his eyes and didn't reply.

When he got in his car, he reminded himself to drive to Aaron's house, not his own, and when he finally pulled up, Aaron's car wasn't there. While he waited, he checked his phone, seeing another message from Rod.

You're all good, Zaire. What are friends for if you can't let the barriers go once in a while? Make sure you talk things through with Aaron. He seems like a nice guy. Let me know how you are when you get five.

Zaire replied as Aaron pulled into the driveway.

I'm good. I'm at Aaron's now. We briefly spoke this morning and things seem okay between us. I'll let you know if it changes. I'm not planning on being home tonight, so I'll message you again tomorrow. Thanks for everything last night. Especially taking me to

**Aaron's, even if it was because you didn't
want to look after me, lol.**

His phone buzzed again as he climbed out of his
car, and he smiled at the middle finger salute Rod
replied with.

"You look happy."

Zaire grinned up at Aaron. "Just messaging Rod.
He's an idiot sometimes, but a lovable one."

"He seemed nice when I met him last night."

The reminder of the previous evening tensed
Zaire's muscles, knowing what was going to happen
when he entered Aaron's house, even if he didn't know
the specifics.

"Come on in. Hang your stuff up and follow me to
the kitchen."

Zaire did as asked without replying. When he
entered the kitchen, Aaron was busy preparing some
food and placed a plate with some fruit slices, a
yoghurt and a glass of milk in front of Zaire.

"Eat up. I don't want you passing out from hunger
if you can't last until dinner." Aaron chuckled as he
said it.

Zaire ate his food, surprisingly hungry, though he
didn't usually eat straight after work. When he finished,
Aaron took the plate from him and rinsed it before
coming back to sit next to Zaire.

"Alright. I don't usually delay punishments, but
because of yesterday's events, I had to. Do you
remember what you did yesterday that you need to be
punished for?"

Zaire nodded and kept his gaze on his hands, which surrounded the chilled glass. "I was being naughty at the staff meeting."

"Yes. But I am also going to punish you for scaring the hell out of me last night. When I couldn't get hold of you, I was worried something had happened to you. No one would have thought to let me know if you'd been in an accident." Aaron took Zaire's hand. "You scared me, sweetheart."

Zaire had never thought about that. He wrapped his other hand around Aaron's. "I'm so sorry, Daddy. I didn't think."

"No, you didn't. I know you were hurt, but you should have come to me with your questions. I'm here for you, no matter what you have to say. Even if it hurts me, I want you to tell me. I want to be able to make it better."

"I should have. I know now, but at the time, I was so upset and afraid I'd made a mistake."

"I understand. But you should have spoken to me about it. Even if I had told you what we had was a fling, wouldn't it have been better to know than to wonder?"

Zaire thought about it and realised Aaron was completely right. Despite the fact he would have to ask an uncomfortable question, Zaire would have known straight away, and none of this would have happened.

"I suppose I have a lot to learn about relationships."

"No. You have a lot to learn about our relationship. There is a difference. Our relationship will be different from any other relationship you have. That is one of the amazing things about having a Daddy and boy lifestyle."

Zaire said nothing. He couldn't disagree.

"Now, onto your punishment."

Zaire swallowed hard but didn't move his gaze away from Aaron's. "Yes, Daddy," he said solemnly.

"Go into the living room and sit on the chair in the corner, facing the wall. I expect you to stay there for thirty-five minutes. While you are there, you need to think about why you did what you did. I have my own ideas, but we'll discuss it afterwards."

"Yes, Daddy." Zaire stood and gave a small smile before heading to the living room. He didn't like the idea of sitting there alone for the next half an hour, but he would. He deserved it for what he'd put his Daddy through yesterday.

There was a wooden chair with arms, not particularly comfortable, and it faced the corner where there was nothing he could see except beige-coloured wallpaper. There was nothing to distract him from the time. And the time crawled.

He could do nothing but think, and it irked him something rotten. He liked being busy and getting things done, but here he couldn't do anything except fidget. Staring down at his shoes, Zaire thought about yesterday. He hated being a secret. It was that simple. He wanted a relationship he could shout to the rooftops about, not one he had to pretend didn't exist when he was at work but was full and bountiful when work finished. It wasn't fair he couldn't have it all.

Zaire frowned. How could they make it work? If he couldn't deal with it like it was, he either needed to find a new job, or he needed to leave Aaron. His pulse stuttered at the thought, and he knew there was no way he'd be able to leave Aaron. Even his stupidity of the night before didn't change the fact he was falling for his headteacher. In fact, it exacerbated it. He reacted that way because he didn't want to lose Aaron and thought he had no choice. Now, though, he would fight for them. So, the best idea would be to find a new job. He hated letting Aaron and Uma down, but it was for the best.

"Zaire?"

Zaire jumped but didn't remove his gaze from the wall. His Daddy hadn't told him he could move, yet. Aaron came around the front of the chair and crouched down.

"You've done so well, my precious boy. I'm so proud of you." Aaron rose and pressed his lips to Zaire's, licking across them to request entry, which Zaire would never deny. Aaron pulled away, leaving them both breathless, and lifted Zaire's hands to help him to his feet.

"Let's get changed and watch some TV before I have to go and make dinner."

Zaire smiled, and Aaron dressed him in what he called his comfort clothes—shorts, vest and robe—and he settled on the sofa to watch Tom and Jerry. He knew Aaron had left the room at one point but was too engrossed to wonder why.

"Time for dinner."

As soon as Aaron said it, Zaire could smell the spicy scent in the air, which he hadn't noticed before. Aaron led him to a chair at the kitchen table, pushing his chair in when he was seated. Zaire watched him as he pottered around, gathering plates and cutlery and adding finishing touches to the food before bringing over enchiladas.

"Mmm, smells delicious. Thank you, Daddy."

"You're very welcome, sweet boy." As they ate, Aaron brought up their topic for discussion. "So, did you think about what happened yesterday?"

Zaire nodded but didn't answer until he finished his mouthful. "I did. I don't want to be a secret. I don't like pretending I'm not yours." He wasn't touching on the Simon thing.

"That's what I thought, too. I think you were being bratty yesterday because you wanted my attention but were unable to have it because we're keeping things quiet. We need to figure out the best way to work together and be happy with the situation. Both of us happy with the situation."

"I can't see how we can without either telling people about us or me finding somewhere else to work." Zaire was silent for a moment. "I'm going to stay with the agency for a bit longer. See if I can find a job at another school nearby."

Aaron tilted his head. "Are you sure? I don't want you to have to leave somewhere you're happy to work. I know you've been looking for somewhere permanent. If you want to stay at this school, you're welcome to. Although a personal relationship is allowed within the school, we need to think about the bigger picture regarding parents and governors. It will prove tricky and will possibly test us, both as a relationship and as a boss and employee, but I think we are strong enough to handle it, don't you?" Aaron smiled at him.

"I would like to think we are. But it's for the best for me to find somewhere else. I'm sorry for leaving as soon as I agreed. I will stay at the school until you've found a replacement."

"It's not a problem. And thank you for staying to help. I will find someone as soon as I can. I think we should tell Pamela and Uma about our relationship; that way, each of us has someone who we can talk to if needed while I find a new teaching assistant. They are our friends, after all." Aaron smiled.

"Okay, Daddy." Zaire couldn't feel any effects of the alcohol anymore, yet he was shattered, but if he slept, he wouldn't get to see Aaron much. He wanted to spend as much time as possible with Aaron.

"Have you finished your dinner, sweetheart?"

"Yes, thank you." Zaire yawned.

"Let's get you ready for bed. You need your rest."

"But it's only six!"

"Well, I was going to suggest watching TV before bed, but I think maybe you need some more time in the time out chair." The tone was short and sharp.

Zaire ducked his head. "No! I hate that chair!"

"I think you're tired, Zaire, and you need sleep."

"I don't want to go to sleep yet! I want to spend more time with you."

"As sweet as that is, you need sleep," Aaron reiterated.

Zaire stood, scraping the chair back on the floor. "Fine. I'll go to bed, then." He stomped to the stairs, jogging up them and heading straight to the bed. Flopping down on the covers, he closed his eyes, all the fight leaving his body. Tears escaped from his eyes. He hated disappointing his Daddy, but he also hated not being able to be with him. He rolled to his side and gripped the pillow in his hands as his tears came. He felt the bed dip behind him and arms come around his waist.

"Let it all out, Zaire. I'm here for you, sweetheart. I'm not going anywhere."

Zaire twisted around and wrapped his whole body around Aaron's, face pressed into his chest as his tears soaked into Aaron's shirt. He had no idea how long it had been when he finally relaxed enough to think clearly. He took a deep breath.

"Sorry, Daddy," he whispered.

"It's okay, sweet boy. We will figure this all out. But we won't be able to do it when we're tired. We both need sleep, not just you. I didn't get much last night either. I thought if we both had an early night, we would feel better tomorrow and could think clearly about what to do. I should've explained it to you."

"It's okay."

"It's not okay. I want communication from you, but I also need to remember I need to communicate with you, too. It's not fair for me to expect you to behave in certain ways if I haven't explained how or why." They laid in silence for a few moments before Aaron moved.

"We need to get ready for bed, or I'll be asleep like this." He chuckled.

Zaire smiled and sat upright. "I think sleep is a good idea."

Aaron stroked a hand over Zaire's head. "After some sleep, we'll be able to fight the whole world if we have to."

"We will, Daddy, but I hope we don't have to."

CHAPTER TWELVE

AARON

Aaron had been correct when he'd told Zaire that Pamela and Uma wouldn't care about their relationship—not their Daddy and boy relationship, just that they were in one.

Zaire had spoken with the agency and agreed to stay on at the school until a replacement could be found. Aaron got right on it as soon as he'd set foot in the office that morning. He had several interviews set up for the following week.

When Friday finally rolled around, Zaire had asked if they could go to the club. Aaron wanted nothing more than to sit it out after the week he'd had, but he'd agreed. He didn't want Zaire getting the idea Aaron didn't want to be seen with him.

They planned to go to Infinity, and Zaire had invited Colin, who was still with Dave, and Rod, who was alone because his girlfriend was away with her friends, and Aaron had invited Nora, Geoff and Cord. It was turning into a get-together. Aaron was glad Zaire had suggested it because it would give their friends the chance to meet and mingle. There was one thing on Aaron's mind.

"Zaire?"

"Yes, Daddy."

"When we're out, what do you want to be? Do you want to be Zaire or my boy?"

Zaire tilted his head, and Aaron could see him working through his options. "Your boy, please, Daddy."

"You sure?"

Zaire nodded, a grin stretching across his face.

"In which case, I have something for you." Aaron's heart raced as he headed to his bag to fetch his newest acquisition. He'd been carrying it around for the last few days, not sure when or if to offer it. Lifting the box out, he twisted back to face Zaire. "You don't have to wear this, but I would very much like it if you did because you'd be seen to be mine."

Zaire's brow creased until Aaron opened the hand-sized box. Nestled inside was a beautiful, amber-coloured collar that matched Zaire's eyes. The eyes which widened as he stared. Zaire's hand reached forward, and his fingers brushed against the collar in an almost reverent action.

"If you don't like it, you don't have to w—"

"I love it, Daddy!" Joy spread across Zaire's face, his eyes sparkled, his cheeks flushed, and he did a happy dance on the spot. "Can I wear it now?" he asked, hope blossoming in his eyes.

"You can wear it whenever you want to," Aaron answered, his heart expanding at the obvious excitement coming from Zaire.

"Please, Daddy! Now, please!" He clapped his hands together, and Aaron beamed.

He released it from the box and, placing the box on the top of the drawers, unfastened it before beckoning for Zaire, who came willingly. As Aaron fastened it around Zaire's throat, something inside him unclenched at the obvious ownership on Zaire's body. He felt like he had someone who he could share his life with. Someone who could help him as much as Aaron helped his boy. Once it was fastened, he ran his fingers across it and Zaire's skin.

"You look fantastic," Aaron breathed.

Zaire smiled, looking at him from underneath his lashes. "Will you help me choose what to wear, please, Daddy?"

"Of course, my boy. Do you have any ideas, or do you want me to choose for you completely?"

"Can you choose, please?"

"Of course. Go wait by the bed, and I'll be there in a few minutes."

Zaire sneakily lifted to his feet and planted a kiss on Aaron's lips before skipping off across the room. Aaron shook his head, smiling. He always felt so much lighter when Zaire was around. He made the world appear filled with brighter colours.

Deciding to choose a top for him first, he opened

the wardrobe and rifled through the options. He came across a black halter-neck with a golden shimmery overlay, which he thought would look amazing with the collar. He checked out the options for Zaire's legs. There were skirts, dresses, trousers, shorts and probably other items Aaron had no idea about. He saw some white trousers and pulled them out, realising they were three-quarter length ones. They'd look great with the top and some heeled or flat shoes, depending on what Zaire wanted to walk in.

Heading over to Zaire, who stood at the foot of the bed, a dreamy gaze on his face as he stroked his collar, Aaron lay the clothes on the bed. Smiling at Zaire, he diverted to the drawers and opened the top, looking for nude-coloured underwear. He found a thong and plucked it out, hanging it from his finger as he pivoted towards Zaire once more. This time, Zaire's heated gaze was on Aaron.

Aaron wandered over to him, his gaze taking in every inch of Zaire that was exposed to him. Which was considerable as Zaire had finished in the shower and wore a small towel. As he stepped close enough to touch, he rested his fingertips on Zaire's chest, slowly skimming them lower as Aaron kneeled in front of him. They were going to be late meeting their friends.

His fingers slid over the growing bulge in the towel and down his calves to his feet, where Aaron tapped for Zaire to lift so Aaron could slide on the thong. When he lifted the thong up Zaire's legs, he made sure to skim his fingers over the skin along the way. As he reached the bottom edge of the towel, Aaron glanced up at Zaire and raised an eyebrow in an unsaid question. Zaire swallowed hard and opened his mouth as he exhaled in a rush before moving his hands to the knot in the towel. He undid it and dropped it to the floor next to them.

Unable to help himself, Aaron pressed a kiss to the erect cock right in front of him, and Zaire moaned. Aaron continued to lift the thong into place, leaving Zaire's cock poking out the top of the waistband but sliding his finger between his ass cheeks to ensure the back of it was in place. To do it, he had to get closer to Zaire's shaft, and Aaron lapped at the exposed head to the music of Zaire's harsh breathing.

"Fuck, Daddy! Please, don't leave me like this!" Zaire begged so beautifully.

Aaron brought one hand to the front and used one finger to pull Zaire's cock away from his stomach, giving Aaron more space. He took the head of Zaire's shaft into his mouth and lightly sucked, using his tongue on the underside. The hand that remained in Zaire's crack moved higher and pressed against his hole, eliciting a moan and a thrust forward and back, like Zaire couldn't decide which he wanted more.

As he hadn't used any lube, Aaron pulled his hand away and lifted it to Zaire's mouth, all the while suckling at his tip, playing with the tiny slit in the head and the extremely sensitive underside. Zaire's cock was now rock hard and barely constrained in the lacy thong. When he deemed his fingers wet enough, he removed them from Zaire's mouth and returned to his hole. Sliding more easily now, he pressed a little harder against the entrance to his passage. Aaron felt when Zaire relaxed because his finger slid past his muscle ring, and Zaire groaned.

"Oh god, please let me come." Zaire thrust between the two sensations, his rhythm faltering as he neared the precipice.

Not wanting this to be over quite yet, Aaron pulled away, and Zaire's legs wobbled. Aaron held Zaire's hips as Aaron stood, taking Zaire's mouth in a carnal, rough kiss and pushing him back onto the bed, all the while keeping their lips locked. Zaire spread his legs to allow Aaron room.

While bracing one hand beside Zaire's head, Aaron used his other to undo his jeans, pushing them down enough to free his cock. He grasped both shafts in his hand and stroked. They both groaned into the kiss as their hips thrust into his tight fist. Aaron's tongue mimicked the movement of his hips, and Zaire sucked on it, hurtling them towards the end.

Aaron pulled his mouth free, gasping for air. Gazing down at Zaire, he saw his pupils had blown wide enough to almost cover the amber colour of Zaire's eyes, his lips were ruby red and bruised, and his cheeks were flushed. Aaron tightened his grip, wanting to watch as Zaire flew. Zaire's mouth opened further, air audibly inhaled and exhaled as he reached for his climax. Zaire's back bowed, his nostrils flared, and Aaron told him to come.

"Fuck!" Zaire shouted as his release coated his stomach and chest, followed closely by Aaron's.

"God, yes! Fuck, Zaire!" Aaron growled as his climax roared through him, marking Zaire as his.

Aaron rolled to his back next to Zaire, breathing as if he'd run a marathon. Their hands threaded together as they lay there, regaining their equilibrium.

"I can't move," Zaire mumbled.

Chuckling, Aaron sat up. "You don't need to for the moment. Let me clean you up." He rose to shaky legs, locking his knees so he didn't fall back to the bed, even though it was where he wanted to be. Looking down at himself, he snorted.

"What, Daddy?"

Aaron glanced at Zaire. "I'm still fully dressed." He turned to show Zaire only his cock stuck out from his undone jeans, every other item of clothing was in place.

Zaire put a hand over his mouth as laughter danced in his eyes. "You look hot," he whispered.

Aaron leaned over the bed to move Zaire's hand and press a kiss to his lips. Their cocks slid against each other, and they groaned into the kiss before Aaron pulled away.

"I'll clean you up and get you dressed. We're going to be late as it is." Aaron grinned at Zaire, a lightness in him he had not felt for so long.

After cleaning Zaire up, Aaron pulled the lace over his cock.

"Are you not going to change the thong, Daddy?" Zaire's voice was shaky, and Aaron gazed up at him, seeing Zaire's frown.

He supposed some people didn't like wearing

underwear they had come in, but neither of them had spilled anything on the lace. "No, sweet boy. I want you to remember what we did whenever you go to the bathroom and see this lacy thong. I promise you, they are clean, they…" Aaron leaned forward, pressing his nose into the fabric and inhaling, "smell like you and me," he finished on a growl.

As his gaze returned to Zaire, he saw his pupils dilate and knew they needed to get moving; otherwise, they would end up in bed again, and Aaron didn't want Zaire to miss out on his night out.

The clothes he'd picked for Zaire rested next to them, untouched by their previous actions. He helped Zaire stand and reached for the trousers, pulling them up his legs and over his ass before fastening them. They moulded to Zaire's thighs as if they were made especially for him. Aaron stood, grabbed the top and helped Zaire into it. As he thought, it highlighted the collar beautifully, and Aaron couldn't help but take Zaire in a long, deep kiss as his hands caressed the leather band.

"God, you're amazing, Zaire." He rested their foreheads together as he regained his breathing once more. "And you're dangerous." He chuckled and blew out a breath. "What shoes would you like to wear tonight?"

Zaire blinked at him a few times before seemingly shaking off his lust. "Um, I have some low wedge shoes which would work."

"Okay. Go grab them, and I'll help you."

In no time, Zaire was finally fully dressed, and they

were on their way to the club—forty-five minutes late, but on their way, nonetheless.

As they entered the club, Aaron gripped Zaire's hand tight, not wanting to lose him amongst the Friday night crowds. They weaved their way around the bar, trying to find any of their friends and finally noticed Cord waving at them from a table near the back.

"What took you so long?" Cord yelled to be heard over the music.

Aaron glanced at Zaire, seeing a flush colour his cheeks. "We got waylaid."

"Yeah, you got laid, alright," Cord answered with a grin.

Aaron ignored him and pulled Zaire down onto one of the two spare seats at the large table they'd commandeered. Zaire introduced him to Rod and Colin again, and Aaron introduced Zaire to Nora and Geoff, who Zaire had not met properly yet. Once everyone knew everyone, Aaron waved down a waiter and ordered a round of drinks.

"So, how are things going?" Nora asked him, leaning past Cord to ask in a quieter voice.

Aaron grinned. "Really well."

"That's all you're going to give us?" Cord asked.

"Yep."

"You're an asshole."

"What more do you want? I'm not giving you a play by play of our activities." Aaron shook his head.

Nora laughed. "I see you have collared him, but have you hit the bump yet?"

Aaron glanced across at Zaire, seeing him in

animated conversation with Rod, Colin and Dave, and focused back on Nora and Cord. "Yes. You know we had a bit of an issue on Monday, but with Rod's help, it got sorted quickly."

Nora raised her eyebrows. "You know that's not the bump I meant."

Clenching his jaw, Aaron grabbed his beer and took a long gulp. He knew exactly what she meant. In any new relationship, there seemed to be a general bump several days or weeks into it, where the boy debated whether he was with the right Daddy, or happy where he was, or something similar. Most other Daddies or Mummies he knew of had witnessed or experienced the same thing, just in different ways. He had hoped their differences on Monday was their 'bump,' but Nora made him reconsider. Zaire had taken everything so well, except for the Simon issue, but they got through it. He hoped Zaire would talk to him if he had any second thoughts about them.

CHAPTER THIRTEEN

ZAIRE

Aaron became quiet as the night wore on. Zaire wondered what had been said for him to retreat, but every time Zaire checked in with him, he'd smiled and said he was fine. Now, heading to Zaire's house in a taxi, Aaron was gripping Zaire's hand and staring out of the window as if all the answers of the world were out there.

Zaire had a fantastic night. He'd gotten to know Nora and Geoff, who were great, and Cord, who was a bit of an asshole, but he could imagine would be a wonderful Daddy to some boy. He'd been able to catch up with Colin, too. He was enjoying his time with Dave, and Zaire had double-checked he was happy, which he was. As for Rod, Zaire had hugged him to thank him for taking him back to Aaron on Monday. Although they had spoken throughout the week, Zaire hadn't seen him since and owed him a lot.

But his night had been overshadowed by Aaron's silent behaviour. The only thing Zaire could think of was someone had said something to him, and it worried Zaire. He didn't want someone to warn Aaron away from him. He'd just found his Daddy; he didn't want to lose him again.

The worry had him resting his head on Aaron's shoulder and wrapping his free arm around Aaron's biceps, trying to get as close as he could without mounting him.

A hand came up and stroked his hair. "Are you okay, sweetheart?"

"Uh-huh," he answered. He wasn't sure how to explain what he was feeling, although he needed to try because they promised communication between them. It meant Aaron needed to talk, too. He kept silent until they got to his place. "Daddy?" he said when they were in the kitchen, Aaron grabbing some water.

"Yes, sweet boy." Aaron smiled across at him.

"You said we needed to talk to each other—to communicate."

"Yes?" Aaron said when Zaire didn't continue.

"What's wrong, Daddy? You've been quiet all night. Did I do something wrong?" He stood there, wringing his hands together, not wanting to bring it up but needing to all the same.

Aaron rubbed a hand over his mouth and beard before answering, "No, Zaire. You've done nothing wrong." He sighed, shoulder slumping. "It's…Come on, let's go sit for a minute. I'll explain what was said."

They moved to the sofa, and Aaron lifted his arm

so Zaire could snuggle up against him. Zaire took some comfort in the fact Aaron was not pushing him away, at least not physically.

"In many Daddy or Mummy relationships, there is a point when the boy or girl begins to doubt what they have together is true. We call it 'the bump.' Most bumps are minor, and everyone carries on as normal afterwards, but sometimes, the bump ends the relationship."

"And you're worried we haven't hit my bump yet?"

Aaron nodded. "Nora reminded me about it tonight, and it got me thinking. Monday was a bump, but I don't think it was one which could potentially make you reconsider what we have."

Zaire sat upright. "I don't think I'm going to have a bump, Daddy. I really don't. Monday made me realise I want you in my life. I want everything with you. No one has ever made me feel like you do. Haven't we already been through so many ups and downs?"

"Yes, we have. I want you to be happy, that's all. And if it ends up that I don't make you happy, I'll accept it, but I won't like it."

Zaire moved, straddling Aaron and bringing their faces closer together. "I can't predict the future, but as of this moment in time, I can honestly say I have never been happier." His hand trailed across his collar as he gave Aaron a beaming smile.

Aaron's melancholic expression lifted, and Zaire leaned in for a kiss, resting his hands against his Daddy's beard, feeling the scratchy texture tickle his palms. Their kiss was languid, and Zaire got lost in the sensations, his brain completely switching off from anything not related to the feel of Aaron beneath and around him.

As Zaire's arousal increased, he rocked his hips against Aaron, the friction barely there and not quite enough. Aaron gripped his waist, stilling his movements and pulling away from his mouth.

"Are you trying to take something you didn't ask for?" Aaron growled, his voice significantly deeper than usual.

Zaire's eyes widened as he flicked through his options. He could deny thrusting against Aaron and be guaranteed a punishment of some sort, and possibly not a good one, or he could admit it and possibly get a good punishment for being honest. The longer he stared at Aaron, the less sure he was of his best choice.

"Well?" Aaron prompted.

"Sorry, Daddy. I wanted some relief. I didn't think about what I was doing. I'm sorry." Zaire stared at Aaron's shirt as he waited for the verdict, hoping he had been apologetic enough to warrant some sort of reward.

"Okay, sweet boy, but remember in the future, you need to ask for what you want. As you were so impatient, we are heading to bed now, without any relief. For either of us."

"But—" Aaron's raised eyebrows halted his words, and Zaire bit his lip.

When Aaron pushed against Zaire and helped him stand, then followed suit, Zaire moped, keeping his gaze on the floor as he trailed behind his Daddy up the stairs. He was annoyed because all he wanted to do was feel Aaron sliding deep inside him and pounding him into the mattress. They'd been together for a while now, and they'd still not had sex. He had hoped to get Aaron aroused enough to finish the night off with a bang. Zaire had to go and ruin it by being impatient. He kept trying to remember that his Daddy knew best, but it was difficult. Even though he wanted someone to look after him, it was hard to let the reins go after being alone for so long.

"I don't think we need a shower before bed, but would you like one?" Aaron turned the bedside lights on, filling the room with a warm glow. Zaire loved that, even though it was Zaire's house, Aaron had made himself comfortable enough to take care of Zaire. Aaron didn't hesitate to do what he needed to do to make sure Zaire was looked after.

"I'm okay, thank you."

"Let's get you undressed. Are your feet sore from the shoes?" Aaron crouched down to undo the buckles and slip each shoe off Zaire's feet.

Zaire groaned and scrunched and flexed his toes into the carpet now they were out of their confines. "They are a little, but nothing I'm not used to."

Aaron helped Zaire remove his other clothing until he was stood naked in the middle of the room as Aaron chose something for him to wear. He pulled out a chemise Zaire rarely wore. It was light pink silk with thin straps and a lace detail across the chest. He glanced over at Zaire as if to gauge his reaction, but Zaire honestly didn't mind what he wore. Nodding his head, Aaron closed the drawer and stepped up to him.

"Arms up."

The material flowed down his skin, making him feel small and sexy, and he couldn't help but run his hands over the texture and sigh.

"You look gorgeous."

"Thank you, Daddy."

"You're welcome." He pressed a kiss to Zaire's lips. "Let's get this collar off."

Zaire's hand instantly went to the leather strap. "Can't I keep it on?" he asked, his heart racing.

"It's probably not a good idea. I don't want you to get a sore neck." Zaire pouted, his shoulders slumping. Aaron must have seen Zaire was upset because he added, "But how about if we take it off and put it right next to you on the bedside table so you can see it at any point and put it on straight away in the morning?"

Zaire mulled it over. He didn't want to take it off, but he knew Aaron was right. "Okay, Daddy."

The buckle came loose easily enough, and soon Zaire felt a loss he hadn't expected when Aaron first encased his neck in the warmed fabric. He'd truly felt like he belonged to Aaron when he was wearing it and, strangely, a little lost without it. He watched as Aaron walked over to the bedside table and placed it where he'd said he would. Zaire didn't like it, but at least it was within reach.

"Come to bed." Aaron held out his hand after flicking the cover back. Withholding his smile, Zaire sashayed over, a larger sway in his hips than he would usually make and made sure to brush against Aaron as he slid past him.

A chuckle met his ear as he climbed onto the soft, cool sheets, laying on his side so he could see the collar. It might seem silly to some that he was scared it would be taken away, but he'd never had one before. None of his previous Daddies had ever given him one. Whenever they had gone out to clubs or bars, they always kept him with them, and he hadn't been able to go and dance with his friends without them being there, too. The collar, although giving him a sense of being owned, also gave him more freedom as he was able to dance and go to the bathroom without anyone getting in his face because it proved he belonged to someone.

When he was tucked in, Aaron leaned down and pressed a kiss to his forehead. "Sleep, my sweet. I'm going to get undressed, and I'll be with you."

Zaire nodded, his blinking getting heavier, even though he tried to keep his eyes on his collar.

↔

Zaire woke with his ass pressed against Aaron's groin, Aaron's deep breathing heating his neck and whispering past his ear. He wanted nothing more than to rub back against him, but his eyes snagged on his collar, and he remembered his Daddy's words from the previous night. Gritting his teeth against the need to move, he inhaled, hoping to calm himself.

"Daddy?" he whispered. When he received no

answer, he lifted the hand Aaron had curved around Zaire's waist and pressed a kiss to his fingertips. "Daddy?" he said again, cuddling the hand against his chest, fighting against the urge to thrust his hips. He wasn't sure how much longer he could hold himself together.

"Hmm, good morning, sweetheart." Aaron's voice rumbled, husky and deep, into his back as his nose rubbed circles on Zaire's neck. He pressed a kiss to his spine. "Do you need something?"

"Please, Daddy. I've been so good. I woke you up to ask you instead of moving like I wanted to! Please can you make me come? I'm so hard," he whispered the last bit, a flush heating his cheeks at his admission.

"Oh, is my sweet boy needing his Daddy?"

"Yes, please!"

Aaron disentangled his hand from Zaire's grasp and smoothed it down Zaire's front using his fingertips, grazing across his silk-covered skin. Aaron trailed over Zaire's nubs, causing Zaire to buck his hips and gasp as a tingle was felt in his cock. An arm slid under Zaire's neck, and Aaron pulled Zaire back against him, wrapping an arm across his chest as his other hand continued its journey.

"Look at me, sweetheart."

Zaire rolled his head to the side and met Aaron's kiss in a fierce, hungry clash of lips and tongues. Zaire's eyes closed on a moan when Aaron's hand closed around his dick. Zaire rocked his hips back and forth into Aaron's hand and against the hard cock pressed against his crack. Needing a breath, Zaire twisted his head away, panting and gripping the sheets beneath him as his hips moved faster. He was so close.

Aaron pulled away, and Zaire whimpered as his rise to orgasm stuttered and dropped. He heard a scrape and a rustle, and Aaron was back. Zaire glanced over his shoulder and saw Aaron rolling on a condom and opening a tube to slick his cock and his fingers. Aaron threw the tube to the side, spooning Zaire once more, his arm sliding back under Zaire's neck as his lube-free fingers pushed against Zaire's upper thigh. Zaire moved his leg, opening him up to Aaron's questing fingers.

The first pass of the slicked fingers over his hole had Zaire's breath catching in his throat and arching his head backwards.

"I'm going to take care of my boy now," Aaron groaned into Zaire's ear as one finger pressed forward.

Zaire hitched his leg higher, giving Aaron more space to pump into his ass. "More, Daddy! I can take more!"

A second finger joined the first, Aaron taking him at his word. Zaire could feel Aaron's cock resting against his lower back while Aaron prepared him. As a third joined in, Zaire groaned, closing his eyes and felt: every slide of his fingers in his passage, every heated breath against his neck, every area of his body humming with arousal, and the press of Aaron's much larger cock against his hole. Zaire bore down, arching his ass to get closer, to get Aaron inside him quicker.

Aaron took it slow. Short, continual thrusts once he'd passed the tight ring of muscles had Zaire delirious. His eyes rolled back in his head, and Aaron's grip tightened against Zaire's leg as his hips pumped. Sweat coated them. The sound of their bodies coming together was loud in the quiet room, and Zaire loved every minute of it.

His eyes blinked open, gaze snagging on his collar, and his orgasm flared closer. "Wait," he gasped, and Aaron immediately stopped, though didn't pull out.

"What's wrong, sweet boy?" Aaron panted, tension radiating through him.

"My collar."

Zaire felt a kiss press to his spine and, "Can you grab it?"

He reached forward, hooking it with the tips of his fingers and sliding it forward so he could grasp it. He held it up, and, carefully, Aaron took it from him, wrapping it around his neck and buckling it, all the while keeping their hips pressed together so Zaire could feel every inch of him inside him as his collar was fastened back where it should be.

Once it was done, Aaron held him close, kissing his shoulder. "It's perfect for you."

"You're perfect for me," he responded, turning his head for a kiss, which soon turned into a frenzy when Aaron's hips began to move once more.

The collar tugged at Zaire with every movement, with every swallow, and he loved the reminder of who he belonged to, and it increased his arousal. He was right on the precipice when Aaron canted his hips.

"Oh, fuck! Yes, Daddy! Can I come? Please! I'm so

close." He rambled off more words, or maybe incoherent mumblings, he had no idea.

"God, you feel so fucking good. Yes, sweet boy. Come for me."

Aaron's hips pistoned inside him as Zaire's climax strained his body. His release dragged Daddy's name from his lips, and he felt nothing but pleasure flooding his system. He came back to himself to find Aaron, slowly pumping his hips.

"You with me, Zaire?" he asked.

"Yes, Daddy."

"Good. My turn."

CHAPTER FOURTEEN

AARON

Aaron rolled them so Zaire was almost on his stomach, and Aaron could brace his hands either side of Zaire's chest. One of Zaire's legs was bent, Aaron straddled his other. Once in a suitable position, Aaron withdrew slowly, both groaning, before he slammed his hips forward, Zaire hissing, probably because his sensitive cock brushed against the sheets below him. Aaron thrust repeatedly, watching Zaire watch him over his shoulder. Aaron's climax drew near, and he threw his head back and pressed his hips tightly against Zaire's ass as his orgasm rocked through him. He stayed that way for a few seconds until the tension released him, and he dropped his head to Zaire's shoulder.

"You okay, sweet boy?" Aaron asked.

"Perfect, Daddy."

"Yes, you are." Aaron lifted his head and smiled, leaning forward to kiss Zaire's lips and ending up groaning as his cock pressed further in again. Pulling back, Aaron withdrew and immediately felt bereft. He quickly cleaned them both up and snuggled Zaire back against him on the dry part of the bed with a kiss to the side of his neck, above the collar.

"You like the collar?" he asked, a hint of humour bleeding through his voice.

"Uh-huh. Love it," a sleepy voice answered.

"Sleep, sweetheart. We have all day."

Zaire's soft snores sounded several minutes later, and Aaron grinned. There was no way he'd be able to go back to sleep, even with the warm body next to him, but damn if he was going to move before he had to. The warnings Nora gave him last night were ringing in his ears; even though Zaire reassured him, Aaron couldn't drop the worry completely, but he needed to at least pack it away. Otherwise, he would be obsessing over it and would probably ruin their relationship instead.

With it being Saturday, they had nowhere to be, but after an hour or so, he became restless, so rather than wake Zaire with his fidgeting, he got up and pulled on some joggers. Heading to the kitchen to get some breakfast and a cup of tea, he thought about what to do today. Maybe Zaire would like a trip to the aquarium. It was something adults did as well as children, but if Zaire felt uncomfortable, they could leave. He made a note to ask when Zaire woke. Zaire had mentioned rock climbing, and while it was not Aaron's idea of a good time, he would happily take and watch Zaire. He wouldn't take part himself.

He sat with his toast and tea and grabbed the book he'd already started. He'd not read as much since meeting Zaire, but he was soon lost in the world.

A hand sliding around his shoulders made him jump as engrossed in the fictional world as he was, and he flicked his gaze to Zaire's.

"Hi, Daddy."

"Hi, sweet boy. How are you feeling?" The chemise Zaire had worn last night was in place but with satin underwear and a long satin robe. "You look edible," he growled, feeling his cock perk up.

"Thank you."

Aaron slid his hand around the back of Zaire's neck—and collar—and dragged him into a hot and steamy kiss. Within seconds, he gentled it and nibbled at Zaire's bottom lip before letting go. "Would you like some breakfast?"

"It's okay. I can—" Zaire started, pausing when Aaron raised an eyebrow at him. "I would love breakfast, thank you. I'm sorry. I find it difficult to let go when we're at my house," Zaire admitted as he sat at the table.

Aaron rose and set the toaster going. "I understand, but I love taking care of you. Would you like butter or jam on your toast?" Aaron would bet Zaire wanted jam but would ask for butter.

As a blush tinted his cheeks, Zaire mumbled, "Jam, please."

Aaron beamed at him. "Good boy." He fetched the

jam and some milk from the fridge, rummaging around to find a cup for Zaire to use. Finally, he grabbed a plastic tumbler and half-filled it. He wasn't sure if Zaire went little or just boy and didn't want to push things too far. Usually, he would ask the boy, but he was afraid Zaire would reject everything out of principle, even though he'd had Daddies before. Aaron shook his head inwardly. Ever since Nora had mentioned the bump, he had been second-guessing everything. Although he knew his thoughts might be unfounded, he decided to test the waters with some items and watch Zaire's reactions instead of asking him.

The milk in a child's tumbler, the toast with jam cut into triangles, and an apple cut into slices were placed before Zaire as if he'd had them many times before. Aaron refilled his tea and sat back down as if nothing was amiss.

Out of the corner of his eye, he noticed Zaire hesitate and smile before ducking his head and picking up a slice of toast. When he'd finished his breakfast, Aaron gathered the plates and cup and took them to the sink, returning to Zaire and crouching in front of him.

"You did so well, my sweet boy. I thought we could visit the aquarium today. What do you think?"

Zaire's eyes lit up. "Really?"

Aaron nodded, heart content at giving Zaire what he enjoyed as well as what he needed. "Do you have any toys or colouring here?" He pushed a bit to see if Zaire would admit to wanting to do something.

Zaire stared at Aaron, biting his lip as he considered his answer. Minutely, his head nodded slowly.

Heart racing with the strength of the man seated in front of him, he smiled. "Would you like to play while I clean up?"

Zaire's gaze roamed his face, possibly searching for any hint of disapproval or laughter, before he nodded again.

"Go on. I'll be there in a few minutes." Aaron rose, kissing Zaire's forehead. "Well done for telling the truth."

Zaire ducked his head and snuggled into Aaron, hiding his face in Aaron's chest. "I'm so used to hiding everything. It's difficult to open up after so long."

"I know, sweetheart, and I understand. I'm here to take care of you, to help you be who you want to be, to help us become who we want to be together. I won't make fun of you or be ashamed of you for what you want. You need to tell me, or I'll have to keep guessing."

"Okay, Daddy. I'll try."

"Go on. Go play."

Zaire stepped back and grinned, then pivoted and almost skipped out of the room. Aaron took a moment to lean back against the counter and digest that Zaire was his, at least for as long as Zaire wanted him. He was perfectly imperfect. A boy who needed a Daddy to help guide him. Breathing deeply to deny the sudden onset of happy tears, Aaron turned and washed their dishes before drying and putting them away. Once everything was back to normal, and he believed Zaire had enough time to relax, he grabbed his book and entered the living room.

He smiled when he saw Zaire laid on his stomach on the floor, surrounded by several Postman Pat houses, vehicles and characters. Currently, Zaire was conversing as two of the characters about some missing delivery, complete with voices. The sofa called to him, and he made his way over, making sure to become visible to Zaire so he didn't make him jump. He noticed Zaire pause what he was doing and, when Aaron sat on the sofa and opened his book, went back to playing.

Aaron had no interest in the book at all, he flipped a few pages, allowing Zaire to believe he was reading, but he wasn't. He was watching his boy having fun and being so relaxed. Aaron desperately needed to help Zaire merge the two sides of his personality, but the question was, how?

There were almost three aspects to Zaire's personality: his work demeanour, his sexy clothes one, and his boy, although the sexy clothes and the boy seem to work seamlessly together. Zaire appeared to love wearing the clothes as a boy, too. Maybe Aaron could start by helping Zaire choose different clothes for work. There was certainly no need for him to wear suits. He could choose one of the three-quarter-length trousers or the rhinestone jeans Aaron had seen in there. Or even a lacy top instead of a shirt. It would take a lot more to get him to wear those items, and he wasn't sure if Zaire would fight him on it. Aaron would never make him feel uncomfortable, but there must be a way to help him. A phone call to Nora would be in his near future. Advice was needed from his best friend.

The clock showed it was time to get ready to go. "Time to tidy up, Zaire," he said quietly, not wanting to startle him.

Zaire looked at him, his stress-free face a balm to Aaron's soul. "Is it time for the aquarium, Daddy?"

"Yes, sweetheart. We need to have a shower, get dressed, and we can go."

"Yay!" Zaire scrambled to his knees and packed away the toys into a blue box Aaron had not noticed before, and when Zaire tidied the box into the cabinet, Aaron understood why. He had it hidden from view. "I'm ready, Daddy."

Aaron smiled. "Come on. Let's get cleaned up." He held out his hand for Zaire.

Thirty minutes later, Zaire stamped his foot and crossed his arms. "No, I'm not wearing that."

"Zaire. Is that how you talk to your Daddy?"

"I don't want to wear that top. It looks horrible on me," he whined.

Aaron frowned. "What do you mean it looks horrible. Why?"

"It makes me look skinny like it doesn't fit me properly, and I don't like it!" Zaire yelled the last part, and Aaron had enough.

He strode to the other side of the room and turned the armchair to face the wall. Having remembered

Zaire had complained about this particular punishment before, Aaron decided it was the perfect time to show Zaire who was in charge again.

"Zaire? Sit down here. Now." He waited until Zaire stomped over and dropped himself into the chair, arms crossed. "I will not have you talk to me like that. You will stay here for thirty-five minutes, and when the time is over, you better have something to say to me."

"But—"

"Quiet!"

Zaire sighed, and Aaron went back to the wardrobe. He had no issue with Zaire not wanting to wear certain clothes. He could refuse to wear every item Aaron asked him to, but what Aaron wouldn't tolerate was being spoken to like that. There were better ways for Zaire to make his point. Aaron heard a snuffle from the armchair, and it broke his heart, but he refused to cave.

Aaron shuffled through the clothes that were hanging up, finding a strappy top similar to the halter-neck Zaire had worn the other night, but in white with a silver mesh over the top. He thought Zaire would look amazing in it. He chose some light blue skinny jeans and a white pair of ballet flats to complete the outer ensemble. He went to the underwear drawer and chose something fitting. Laying them all on the bed, he checked the time and sat against the headboard, not wanting to leave his boy alone.

When the time was up, Aaron rose and crouched in

front of Zaire, witnessing the tear tracks left along his cheeks. "Good boy, Zaire."

Zaire threw his arms around Aaron's neck, knocking him backwards and onto his ass with a chuckle. "I'm so sorry, Daddy. I'm so sorry." Zaire repeated it over and over again as Aaron petted his hair and held him tight to calm him.

"It's okay, sweetheart. All done now." He murmured some more words until Zaire loosened his hold.

"I really am sorry, Daddy. I need to use my good words, not my bad ones."

"Exactly. But it's all over now. Let's get dressed. Come see what I've chosen, and if you don't like any of it, let me know calmly."

They rose and wandered over to the bed. Aaron watched Zaire's expression, wanting to catch any unsure looks before they peaked.

"I love it."

Relief flowed through Aaron, and he helped his boy get dressed as he asked some questions about how Zaire wanted to play out the day.

"Do you want to be a boy when we're out or boyfriends?"

Zaire hesitated, biting his lip again. "I've never been a boy in public before. My previous Daddies only wanted it to be at home or clubs."

Once again, Aaron felt like he could throttle those irresponsible Daddies. It seemed Zaire's experiences were less than stellar. "We could always see how it goes.

If you don't feel right, don't, but if it does, go for it. There's no right or wrong answer, Zaire."

"What do you want?"

Aaron measured his words, not wanting to push anything on Zaire. "I would like to be able to take care of you while we are out as well as at home."

"Alright. Can we try? And if I don't like it, then we stop?"

"Of course! Well done for trying, sweetheart. You're so brave. I'm so proud of you."

Zaire blushed and gave a big smile as Aaron helped him with his shoes.

"One more question. Do you want to keep your collar on in public?"

Zaire nodded before Aaron had even finished his sentence. "Yes, Daddy. Definitely."

"Right. I think we're ready to go."

←——————————→

The ride to the aquarium was uneventful, although Zaire had found the website on his phone and got excited about all the different things he read about. The seahorses, starfish and turtles were the favourites going by how often Zaire mentioned them.

Aaron had to keep himself from chuckling the closer they walked to the place after parking the car because Zaire bounced on his feet and talked a mile a minute. At least, until Zaire saw the place. Aaron had honestly thought Zaire had been to the aquarium before, but when Aaron asked him, he'd said he hadn't. When they came upon the large building made from lots of windows, Zaire stopped and stared, mouth open. If it wasn't likely to spoil the moment, Aaron would've taken a photo. Instead, he pulled on Zaire's hand and, as pure unadulterated joy crossed Zaire's face, they entered.

"Oh my god," Zaire whispered, eyes round as he took in everything around him.

Aaron had been many times but tried to see it as though he hadn't. There was a reception area to the left, and to the right was a walkway, which, when followed, would take them to every area of the under-water haven. They would be able to cut in and out to different areas if they wanted to, but Aaron would try and keep Zaire on the winding route, so they didn't miss anything. From where they stood, they could see an enormous, floor-to-ceiling, cylindrical glass tube in the centre of the area, holding a multitude of rainbow-coloured fish.

"Let me go and pay, and we'll head on through, okay, sweet boy," he murmured in Zaire's ear, receiving a distracted nod in return. He kept his eye on Zaire as he waited for his turn and joined him once more, Zaire wrapping his arm around Aaron's biceps. It appeared to be a favourite position for Zaire.

"Come on. The underwater beauty awaits."

Aaron couldn't remember a time when he had smiled so much at the genuine joy and exuberance of someone. Every little thing was magical for Zaire, and he was like a kid on Christmas morning. This was what

Aaron had missed all these years. Taking care of Zaire was amazing, but Aaron also got to see Zaire's awe at experiencing something new…something Aaron had been able to give him. As he watched Zaire, his heart filled more. He knew there was no turning back for him. Not now.

CHAPTER FIFTEEN

ZAIRE

Zaire could not believe how amazing the aquarium was. He had always wanted to go but had never been inclined to go by himself. In some ways, he wished he had gone before because he hadn't realised what he was missing, but in other ways, he was glad because he'd been able to share it with Aaron.

They'd taken a few selfies of themselves in front of different exhibits. It had been a fantastic day, and although they were on their way home, Zaire had loved every tiring minute of it.

He rolled his head on the headrest towards Aaron, watching as he concentrated on the road ahead. "Did you have a good day, Daddy?"

Aaron spared a glance at him and grinned. "I had a wonderful time, Zaire. We'll have to go back again sometime."

Zaire beamed. "Really? I'd love to go back. The

seahorses are so small, I never realised that. And as for their babies, they are so cute," he said in a high, squeaky voice, then giggled. Actually, fucking, giggled. That thought had Aaron snorting and shaking his head.

"What's so funny?"

Zaire sighed, smiling out the window as he thought about the day. "I realised how happy I am. I didn't feel strange when I called you Daddy, and I was able to ignore any weird looks being sent our way. It was nice not to have to worry about anything because I knew you were there to take care of me."

"Yes, I was, and I will continue to if you'll allow me."

Zaire bit his lip. "I'd love that."

$$\longleftrightarrow$$

By Friday morning, Zaire was so calm and content, he didn't even mind getting up early to get ready for work. He'd stayed at Aaron's the previous night, but they'd grabbed some clothes from Zaire's house on the way back from rock climbing, or rather, Aaron had grabbed the clothes. His weekend had been unbelievable: the aquarium on Saturday and rock climbing on Sunday. Zaire's perfect weekend. He'd spent the majority of the time as a boy, letting Aaron do whatever he needed to do to look after Zaire, and he'd spent time watching TV and relaxing with his toys. At several points, Aaron had joined him on the carpet and raced cars around the track or helped build a castle to protect the people from an evil dragon. It had been wonderful. The working week had been a normal week at Aaron's school. It was his last day there because Aaron had found a replacement for him, and although he was sad, he knew he was making the right choice. He didn't want to confuse the lines of their relationship: Daddy and boy, or boss and employee.

"Zaire? Time for breakfast!" Aaron called from the kitchen.

Zaire grinned and raced down the stairs, tightening his robe around his waist as he went and stopped by his chair. "Pancakes!"

Aaron laughed. "Yes, sweet boy. You deserve a good breakfast before work this morning." He checked his watch. "We will have to leave soon, so make sure you eat up, and I'll help you get ready."

"Yes, Daddy." Zaire sat and drizzled some syrup onto his bite-sized pancakes and proceeded to inhale them.

"Woah, slow down there, buddy. You'll make yourself sick." Aaron rested his hand on Zaire's wrist.

Zaire swallowed what was in his mouth before answering, "I thought we were in a rush?"

Chuckling, Aaron replied, "Not that much of a rush! Take your time. I have coffee to drink." He held up his cup. "Don't forget your milk, too."

Zaire gave a closed mouth smile, which no doubt looked like a chipmunk from the food he had stuffed in it, but he didn't care. He felt...carefree. Like he could conquer the world.

After washing his face in the bathroom to get rid of the syrup, Zaire joined a hesitant Aaron in the bedroom.

"I have chosen some clothes, but they're not what you usually wear. Please talk to me—properly—about any issues you have with them." Aaron raised his eyebrow, and Zaire understood his meaning.

Seeing what was spread out before him had Zaire's heart racing. There was a slimline version of the tailored trousers he usually wore, and a cream shirt with lace at the shoulders. He could see Aaron had tried to keep things close to what Zaire usually wore, but now they had a gentler look. There would be no doubt in anyone's mind at work that he liked to wear what he knew they would call feminine clothing. He wasn't sure if he could do it. Memories of his father's words flitted through his head, girl, pussy, weak. He'd avoided receiving those comments by separating himself, and only visiting places he knew would be accepting of what he wore. Anywhere else, he was 'normal.'

"I...I don't know if..." He cleared his throat, staring at the bed.

Aaron wrapped his arms around him from behind. "You can say no, Zaire. I never want to make you feel uncomfortable. But I would like to try and find a happy medium between your work and home lives." Aaron pressed several kisses against the side of his face and neck.

In his mind's eye, Zaire could see how the outfit would look on him, and he realised he wanted to try. It surprised him how much he wanted it. He didn't know if he could, though.

"Can I take a change of clothes with me?" he whispered.

The arms holding him tightened briefly. "Of course, you can. You tell me what you need, and I will make it happen, sweet boy."

Zaire exhaled heavily. "Okay. Let's try this."

Aaron spun him around and pressed their lips together in a quick kiss. "You are so brave. Don't let anyone tell you any different. You deserve the chance to be who you are, Zaire. And I would love to be able to help you get there."

His hands gripped the back of Aaron's shirt as he pressed his cheek against his chest until he remembered they needed to be quick. "Oh, we'll be late!" He pulled away and undid the belt of the robe.

"We're okay, sweetheart. Don't worry."

As Aaron dressed him, Zaire became concerned about the reaction to his clothing, not only from staff but from the children as well. When he mentioned it to Aaron, he simply said, "Tell the children the truth. You like wearing them because they make you feel happy." And if that didn't sum up Zaire's feelings about the matter, nothing did.

He felt tears prick at his eyes, but he refused to let them fall. They were happy tears, but he knew he would worry Aaron. Finally dressed, Zaire stood in front of the mirror and studied himself. He looked good. It seemed strange seeing himself in the clothes but no makeup. He usually wore makeup when he was wearing—what he was now calling—his home clothes, but he felt it was a step too far at that moment.

"Time to go, sweetheart!"

Zaire picked up the bag with his change of clothes and padded down the stairs. He was surprised to find Aaron stood at the bottom, holding a box out. He tilted his head and frowned. "What's this?"

"A gift."

Zaire grinned and placed his bag on the floor. He lifted the lid of the box and moved the tissue paper aside, revealing a beautiful pair of black leather ankle boots with a small heel.

"I knew you didn't have any work shoes to go with your outfit, so I found these. I hope you like them." Aaron's voice sounded unsure, and Zaire stared at him, incredulous.

"I love them! But when…?" He shook his head, returning his gaze to the boots.

"I bought them online and got a quick delivery. I had hoped you'd agree to the clothes I set out for you but didn't want to presume. These would've kept until you were able to take that step." Aaron cleared his throat. "I chose some with only a small heel because I know you are sometimes on the floor with the children and rushing around. I didn't want you to chance falling in higher ones."

"They are perfect, Daddy. Thank you so much!" Zaire took the box from Aaron's hands, placed it down and twined his arms around Aaron's neck. "Thank you," he said sincerely and pressed his lips against Aaron's.

The kiss was bittersweet. Zaire tried to show everything he was feeling in the kiss because he knew he couldn't say the words yet. When the kiss ended, Zaire pulled away and, with a grin, plonked himself on the stairs and slid on his new boots. He knew they might pinch a bit by the end of the day, but he didn't care.

"Come on, my boy. Let's go slay some dragons." With a wink, Aaron opened the front door of his home, and Zaire walked through.

⟵――――――⟶

"Oh my god! You look…" Zaire waited for Uma to finish what she was saying, but his heart raced, and his cheeks flooded with heat. "amazing!" She came to him and embraced him tightly. "I knew there was something inside of you that you kept locked away. I hoped one day you'd have the courage to fly, and I'm thinking Aaron had something to do with this change."

Zaire breathed deeply, flooding his body with much-needed oxygen. "He did."

"Well, I love it. The outfit suits you, and, apart from looking a little pale, you seem lighter."

Grinning, he said, "I feel it, too. I never realised how much holding back was weighing on me. I'm a nervous wreck," he held out his hands to show how much they were shaking, "but I need to do this."

"I agree. You can't live your life hiding, Zaire. What's the point if you do? Be who you want to be, not who you're told to be."

Zaire leaned in and hugged Uma again, pulling away when the next staff member entered, the butterflies starting all over again. When nothing was said, and no snide comments were made, he relaxed once more. He wasn't naïve enough to believe everyone would be as accommodating, but so far, so good.

It was when assembly arrived, he encountered problems.

"What are you wearing?" A voice sneered from behind where he was sat at the side of the big hall.

Zaire glanced over his shoulder, already feeling heat bleed into his cheeks and his muscles clenching with a tension he had hoped would stay gone. Simon was sat, looking him up and down as if he were dog shit on his shoe. Zaire's gaze flicked to the children looking at them with interest from the floor next to them. There was no way they couldn't have heard what Simon had said. He gave them a small smile, turned back towards the front where another teacher was telling a story and swallowed hard, beating back the threat of tears.

"You look like a girl. Is that what you are now? Aaron will hardly go for you if that's what you're trying for."

Zaire ignored the comment, concentrating on the children and the words being spoken from in front of him, not behind. He saw Uma, looking over at him, and she mouthed, "You okay?" to which he nodded and tried for a half-smile. He had no idea whether he managed it or not. Probably not, given the look she returned him.

He stood for their physical activity session, wriggling around and making the kids laugh as they joined in with him.

"God, you're even wearing girly shoes. Jesus Christ," the same voice continued when he returned to sitting.

Zaire honestly didn't know if he could keep the clothes on after Simon's comments. Everyone he worked with in Uma's classroom and all the children had loved what he wore. The children were amazing and had asked lots of questions. Even though what he wore was not feminine, there was a definite softer vibe going on, and the children saw it. He'd done exactly what Aaron had told him to do and explained that the clothes made him feel good about himself and happy, so why shouldn't he wear them? They'd accepted it. One child had even come up to him and whispered, "I want to be a princess when I grow up," and Zaire had hugged him and told him he could be whatever he wanted to be.

When faced with adults, it was a different matter. They were already so set in their ways and beliefs, he knew there was no way he would be able to change their minds about certain things. His choice of clothing one of them. Others had their own stereotypes firmly planted in their heads, and nothing Zaire said would ever change them. He didn't want to in some respects. What he did want was for people to stop thinking it was okay for them to force their opinions on others, especially children. How many times had he heard the phrase, 'Do unto others as you would have them do unto you?'"

Unfortunately, it didn't apply to a lot of people.

As he stood and adjusted his top, getting ready to lead the pupils back to the classroom, Simon's parting comment hurt.

"People like you should not be allowed in schools. I don't need to dress like that to get men."

Zaire bit his lip hard enough to hurt, trying to stem the tears threatening. He would not give in to them when the students were looking to him for guidance. He smiled through his pain, inhaling through his nose and took them back for playtime. His sister's voice aimed at their mother floated through his head, "You're choosing this prissy fag over me and Dad?" As soon as the children were occupied outside with their supervisor, Zaire returned to the classroom.

"Are you okay, Zaire?" Uma came over and draped an arm around his shoulder, rubbing the top of his arm repeatedly in a calming gesture.

"Not really. I need to go and change," he muttered, twisting away from her.

"Why?"

"I can't…do this," he said, throat thick, gesturing to down his body. "I'll be back in a few minutes."

"Zaire, wait!" Uma called after him, but Zaire left the room.

He hustled towards the staff room, wanting to avoid others as much as possible. He refused to break down in front of people he worked with. The closer he got to Aaron's office, which he had to pass to reach the staff room, the easier it was to discern voices.

"—children think, eh? What about the parents when the children go home talking about it? You will have the phone ringing off the hook about this."

"It is none of your concern, Simon." Aaron's voice was tense, and if Zaire was not mistaken, angry.

"What do you mean it's none of my concern. I'm thinking about school. The whole picture. You might want to change things around here, Aaron, but some things will not be accepted."

"I will change things in this school, and you have no choice but to go along with it. For instance, this animosity you have for Zaire is not about how he is dressed, is it?"

Zaire had been about to scamper past the open door but froze with the words Aaron spoke.

"I see how you watch him. You could do so much better."

"You mean you? No, thank you, Simon. I have told you before. I'm not interested."

There was silence for several tense minutes, and Zaire was ready to flee in case one or the other exited the office.

"How can you let him in this school dressed like that! He looks like a girl!"

"No, he doesn't. He looks like a boy. My boy. So, back the fuck off and get out!"

CHAPTER SIXTEEN

AARON

With those words, Aaron flung his hand out, indicating the door. He was fuming. He couldn't remember the last time he had been so angry as he was at that moment. Everything inside and out was vibrating with a wave of fury so strong, he could taste it.

Simon glared at him and marched over to the door, flinging it wide so it banged against the wall loudly and stopped. Standing in the doorway was Zaire, and Aaron had no doubt he had heard enough to be ready to run.

"Zaire? Come here, please." Aaron's voice brooked no argument, although he could see Zaire wanting to. Zaire remained stubbornly where he was, gaze flicking from Aaron to Simon and back again. "Simon, leave. Now! You've done enough today, I think. We will be taking this further."

"You bet your ass I'll be taking this further. Enjoy the time with your girlfriend," he sneered as he slunk past Zaire.

"Zaire!"

Zaire's pained gaze met his, and Aaron wanted to soften towards him, but it was not what Zaire needed right now.

"In my office. Now."

Zaire shuffled forward until he was a step across the doorway, and Aaron withheld a chuckle at the show of obedience versus Zaire's need to run.

"Shut the door and come stand in front of me."

The door clicked shut, the sound loud in the silence. Zaire stepped closer to Aaron, but there was too much space as far as Aaron was concerned.

"Here," he said, pointing to the floor right in front of him. Zaire trailed closer until they were almost toe to toe, and Zaire had to lift his head to look at Aaron. "His words mean nothing. Do you understand?"

Zaire swallowed, his Adam's apple bobbing quickly, but he didn't reply.

"His words mean nothing. Do you understand me?" Aaron reiterated, this time with a raised eyebrow.

Zaire licked his lips, and his nostrils flared. "Yes," he uttered.

"I didn't hear you."

"Yes," Zaire said louder, though Aaron could hear the tremor.

"How did your colleagues react this morning when you entered the classroom?" Aaron made sure to keep their gazes locked. He didn't want to lose Zaire's focus.

"Um…everyone was nice."

"Did anyone say anything horrible to you?"

Zaire shook his head.

"Are you close to those people in your class?"

Zaire nodded. Aaron would allow him the non-vocal answers for the moment.

"If you had to spend time with the people in your class or Simon, who would you choose?"

Zaire's eyebrows lifted, creasing his forehead. "What? My class, of course."

"Why are you letting the words of a man you do not want anything to do with affect how you feel about yourself? Or how you think other people feel about you? You already have the evidence from your class colleagues. And I can't imagine the children saying anything mean to you."

Zaire shook his head, a small smile playing around his mouth. "No, they had a lot of questions, like you said they would, but they were so accepting of it."

"Those are the people whose minds we need to focus on changing. The children. This world needs to grow up believing in themselves, believing they can be whoever they want to be and be accepted. And I believe we need to start with the children here, at this age. Teach them what is unusual, out of the ordinary and make them believe it is 'normal.' I want it so very much." Aaron's passion bled into his words. He hated that people didn't consider others. He wanted a world that was free of prejudice, free of hate, free for every-one. He knew it was a pipe dream, but if he could change even one child's view, he would be happy.

"Thank you."

"Thank you, what?"

Zaire smiled and looked at him from under his lashes. "Thank you, Daddy."

"Better." He wrapped his arms around Zaire's waist and pulled him closer, not caring they could be viewed from the school car park. "Were you coming to see me?"

"Huh?" Zaire's brows drew together.

"You were outside my office. Did you need me?"

Zaire focused on Aaron's shirt. "No. I was coming…to get changed," he admitted softly.

Aaron pressed a finger under Zaire's chin until their eyes met. "And now?"

"Now, I need to get back to the children."

"Good boy."

Aaron closed the remaining distance between their mouths and tasted coffee and Zaire. He wanted nothing more than to take it further than the exploration of Zaire's mouth he had managed before a knock at his door sounded. He pulled away, breathing heavily.

"Yes?" he called.

"Mr Brown, Uma asked me to locate Zaire, but I can't find him. She's worried," Pamela answered through the door.

"You can come in, Pamela."

Zaire moved to pull away, but Aaron tightened his grip on him, restricting the space he could move.

Pamela opened the door, stopping, eyes wide. "Ah, I see." They smirked. "You could have told me you knew where he was." They rested a hand on their cocked hip.

"But I wouldn't be able to revel in his blush, would I?" Zaire pushed away, but Aaron pressed a kiss to his forehead first and allowed him space to leave. "Oh, and Zaire?" He waited until Zaire faced him. "Be a good boy and come see me if you have any more issues, okay?"

"Yes, I will." Zaire turned to leave, but once more, Aaron stopped him, needing the words, despite their audience.

"Yes, what?" he growled.

Zaire's gaze flicked to Pamela, who was standing there silently, then back to him. "Yes, Daddy," he whispered as he turned and fled.

"That wasn't nice," Pamela noted.

"He needed to say it. We both needed him to say it in front of someone at work who cares about us." Aaron hadn't realised how much that was true until he said it out loud. He and Pamela had many discussions in the past about their aligned kinks when Pamela had inadvertently seen something Aaron had been looking at.

"I'm glad I was able to help."

"I need your help again now."

"What's up, boss?"

Aaron chuckled at their response. "I want to know everything about Simon. Simon has been put on my shit list after talking crap about Zaire." At their raised brows, he added, "I would be like this had he said it about anyone."

"I know. I've never heard you swear before."

"Not loud enough for you to hear anyway." He laughed. "Simon is denying Zaire the right to wear what he wants. He wants Zaire out of the school to stop him—and I quote—looking like a girl. I want his head on a platter, Pamela. Nobody is allowed to stop someone from being what they want to be in my school." His voice rose at the end of his sentence, his anger returning tenfold.

"Firstly, calm down. Secondly, I will see to it. Thirdly, speak to Uma. Safety in numbers. Until we have something on Simon other than 'he said, he said,' we need to be careful. You do not want to be sued for wrongful dismissal."

Aaron inhaled deeply, resting his hands on his hips as he stared outside. Pamela was right. He needed to be careful; otherwise, Simon would be staying, and Aaron would be out instead of the reverse.

"Thank you, Pamela."

"Just doing my job," they replied as they exited, closing the door behind them.

Aaron settled himself behind his desk, determined to get some work done before any more distractions happened.

When the clock rolled around to three o'clock, Aaron left his office and headed towards Zaire's class. He would not allow Simon to corner Zaire at any point, and it would give him the chance to have a quick word with Uma.

He entered the class as the children were lining up by the door to be collected. A few children called, "Goodbye,

Mr Brown!" to which he replied with a wave and a smile. At his name, he saw Zaire glance up, blush and return to cleaning up. He headed over to Uma's desk and sat on her chair, waiting while she saw the children to their parents.

"Can I help you, Mr Brown?" Uma asked with a twinkle in her eye.

"Actually, yes," he replied, vacating her chair, indicating for her to sit and seeing her eyebrows rise at his serious tone as opposed to her joking one.

"What's wrong?"

He leaned his hip against her desk, keeping an eye on Zaire as he answered, voice low, "Simon is causing issues. I'm handling it at the moment, but I need your help to keep an eye on Zaire. I do not want it escalating more than what it is now."

"And what is it now?"

"Simon has made his thoughts clear on what he believes is needed at this school, and what is not."

"Asshole," she cursed.

"I'm going to speak to the governors and get their backing, but I want Simon gone. I do not want his words hurting any of my staff."

"Okay. Not a problem."

"Thank you. And I'm pinching your helper." He grinned as he pushed away from the desk. "Zaire? Come on. I need you." In more ways than one.

"But I need…" he trailed off when he saw Aaron's face.

"It's okay, Zaire. We're almost done. And besides, you came in early today," Uma backed Aaron up.

"If you're sure." Zaire looked anything but, though he dropped the toys he held into a box and straightened. "Have a good weekend, Uma."

"You, too. Both of you," she replied.

Aaron left the room with Zaire on his heels after Zaire collected his bag and coat.

"I need to nip to my office to grab some things, and we can head home."

"Okay."

Aaron wanted to get Zaire home so he could spoil him rotten. After the day Zaire had endured, Aaron wanted nothing more than to pamper the hell out of him. And it was exactly what he planned to do.

When they arrived at Aaron's house, he helped Zaire out of the car and held open the door for him. Helping him out of his coat and shoes, Aaron grasped his hand and led him up the stairs to the bedroom. Letting his eyes do the talking, Aaron stripped Zaire and himself, walked him to the bathroom and switched on the water. As he let it warm, he cupped Zaire's jaw, pressing little kisses from his forehead, down his nose and to his lips before sipping from his full lips. Once Zaire had relaxed into him, he pulled Zaire back into the shower and proceeded to wash every inch of his body, paying special attention to the hard to reach places.

Zaire's whimpers were music to his ears, and Aaron dropped to his knees. Taking Zaire's cock in his hand, Aaron aimed it towards his mouth and sucked the head.

"Oh my god!" Zaire's hand came to the back of Aaron's head, resting against it.

Aaron rubbed his tongue along the underside and around, seeking any precome he could find. He lowered his head, taking the shaft further into his mouth, hollowing his cheeks to create suction as he bobbed up and down. The hand against his head gripped tighter as Aaron's ministrations became more focused on getting Zaire off rather than soothing him.

"Daddy!" Zaire called as his body tensed, and he shot his release down Aaron's throat.

The blowjob had been quick and dirty, but the aim was to help Zaire relax, which Aaron believed he had managed because when he stood, Zaire rested back against him like a wet noodle. Aaron proceeded to wash Zaire's cock once more, switched the shower off and dried him before picking him up and carrying him to the bed where he laid him down.

Zaire's eyes were closed, but Aaron knew he wasn't asleep. "I'll be back in a minute, sweet boy."

The whimper Zaire made when Aaron stepped away made him want to wrap himself around Zaire in the bed, but he had other plans. He grabbed some joggers from his bag and slid them on, ignoring his half-hard cock and stepped to the drawer of under-wear and gorgeous things Zaire—and Aaron—loved so much. He picked out a silk vest and shorts combo and Zaire's favourite robe before stalking back to the bed. Zaire was lying on his back, but his breathing was more even than it had been.

"I'm here, sweetheart," he whispered. He pressed

his hand gently against the bed next to Zaire's ankle, advertising where exactly he was so he didn't make Zaire jump and moved his hand to Zaire's shin. "I'm going to help you get dressed now."

The shorts were hooked over Zaire's feet and skimmed up his legs with minimum movement required from Zaire, but Aaron needed him to lift his hips. Zaire mumbled something which Aaron didn't catch but lifted, and Aaron slid them into place, running his hand across the front of them—and Zaire's spent cock.

"Let's sit you up, now." Aaron's slipped one arm underneath Zaire's back, helping him to a sitting position. Zaire's eyes were open but unfocused, the kind of look you get when you want to go to sleep but have to wake up. "Lift your arms." Zaire followed Aaron's instructions slowly. The vest was settled into place, and Aaron crouched in front of him. "We'll put your robe on, and you can go and play for a bit while I make dinner. How does that sound?"

Zaire gave a dozy smile and nodded. "Great, Daddy."

When Aaron had settled Zaire in the living room with his Postman Pat toys and cars, he hesitated by the door to the kitchen, looking back at the boy who had changed everything. In such a short time, Zaire had become everything to him. He didn't want this to be a short-term relationship. He was in it for the long-haul, and his need to keep Zaire safe was growing by the second, especially with what happened with Simon that day.

As Zaire sped the cars around the toy town, Aaron's mind was on their next steps—his next steps. Unless he could get more evidence of Simon's discrimination, there was nothing he could do about him without a possible lawsuit being drawn up against him. And Aaron knew he would get hammered in that situation because he had no proof of Simon's wrongdoings. He would take care of Zaire tonight, and they would have a discussion in the morning about the plans going forward. He would have to brace himself for Simon's behaviour to devolve more before he could do anything about it.

Zaire glanced over his shoulder and smiled at Aaron, and his heart soared. There was not much he could do about his need to look after Zaire—he was head over heels in love with him.

CHAPTER SEVENTEEN

ZAIRE

After Aaron had tucked them into bed the night before and wrapped his arms around him, Zaire had lost himself to the oblivion of sleep. His weekend had, once again, been wonderful. Zaire hadn't a care in the world while Aaron had been looking after him. He played with his cars until dinner, which had been homemade macaroni cheese—his favourite—and they settled onto the sofa to watch Top Cat, while Aaron had read. When it had been bedtime, Aaron had led him up the stairs, kissed him hungrily and covered him before sliding in behind him. Zaire had never felt so relaxed, pampered and safe as he had at that moment.

When he woke that morning and realised it was Monday, he worried. He would be visiting a different school that day as his contract with Aaron's school had finished. He was trying to decide whether to continue becoming who he wanted to or stay as he had been for years. He stared at his toast as he chewed what was in his mouth. Aaron finished making his own breakfast and came to sit next to him.

"Are you okay, Zaire?" his Daddy asked.

Zaire took note of his emotions and answered, "I'm nervous. I'm going back and forth about what to wear." He rushed on when Aaron opened his mouth to say something, "I don't want Simon to win by changing who I am, but it's so easy to push myself back in the box, Daddy," he whispered.

"I know, sweetheart. I know. I will support you however you want to do this, but I don't want Simon to dull your shine. And Friday? You shone so brightly because you were true to yourself." Aaron covered his hand with his own and squeezed. "I will support you no matter what you decide to do."

"Thank you, Daddy."

"Finish your breakfast, then we can make all the difficult decisions, alright?"

Zaire nodded because he'd taken a bite of toast. Aaron grinned at him and dug into his food.

Several minutes later, he stood in the centre of his bedroom, wringing his hands in indecision. Aaron stood in front of him, waiting for the answer to his question of what he was going to wear.

"I..."

Aaron rubbed his hands on Zaire's shoulders, calming him. "Whatever you decide," he reminded.

Zaire filled his lungs and blurted, "I want to wear my clothes, not my work clothes."

The smile that crossed Aaron's face made all the

uncertainty worthwhile. Aaron leaned down and pressed a kiss to his lips then stalked to the wardrobe. "I know exactly what you could wear today if you want to. I saw it the other day when I was looking through them."

Zaire's heart was in his throat so he couldn't reply, but he smiled when Aaron looked over his shoulder at him, probably checking he hadn't run out of the room, screaming.

Aaron returned with something purple, and Zaire knew exactly what top it was. He bit his lip in a nervous tick. He knew he would wear it; it was one of his favourites. Aaron pottered around collecting items for a moment until he stood before Zaire once more.

"You okay?"

Zaire nodded, swallowing hard, but beginning to feel more certain about his decision.

"Let's get you ready."

Aaron helped dress him as he usually did, and it helped to centre Zaire even more. Once everything was in place, apart from his shoes, Zaire turned to the mirror. He wore black skinny trousers, ending above his ankle, and a mid-thigh length purple jumper that was also three-quarter sleeved. Zaire tilted his head, approving of the choice, but something was missing. He stepped to his drawers, chose a thin black belt and cinched it around his waist.

Zaire watched as Aaron stood behind him. His hands skimmed from Zaire's shoulders down his arms to link their fingers together. "You look gorgeous," Aaron growled in his ear, nibbling on his lobe. Zaire moved his head to the side as he rested it against Aaron's shoulder, and Aaron kissed down his exposed column. "If it wouldn't be a step too far, I would be marking you here, right now." Aaron licked at the area where his neck met his shoulder, and Zaire shivered. "Come on, my gorgeous boy. Let's show the world who you really are."

Nerves fluttered in his stomach with the words, but Zaire nodded in determination.

By lunchtime, Zaire's stomach was in knots. No one had said anything to him, but he had been getting a few side looks from staff and parents alike. He had to keep reminding himself this was what he wanted, what Aaron believed he was capable of, what he needed to become a whole person; otherwise, he would've changed into something different. Zaire believed in Aaron and that he would help him through this uncertain time. But Zaire also needed to grow a backbone— or rather re-grow his backbone. He never used to be unsure and nervous, but he also never used to merge the two halves of his life. He needed to regain his equilibrium and bring his confidence back. To do that, he needed to make peace with who he was becoming at work.

He loved that he was able to be himself more now, and it was helping him. It was the whispered comments he couldn't hear and couldn't fight against because he didn't know what they were saying. After finishing the pasta salad Aaron had made for him, he stalked to the kettle and made himself a drink. He only had a couple of hours left, and he would be picking

Aaron up from the school. Aaron had wanted Zaire to be there as soon as he had finished.

When he parked the car in the staff car park, as Aaron had told him to, even though he was no longer working there, he got out and leaned against the side of the car, waving to some of the children as they left with their parents.

"Jesus Christ! Did you lose your brain cells along with your masculine clothes? You're not a staff member anymore. Move your car."

Simon's angry voice skated down Zaire's spine, and he clenched his jaw and fists, though didn't respond.

"Have you nothing to say?"

Zaire inhaled shakily. He had plenty to say, but he couldn't say it. Simon wouldn't listen anyway like Zaire's dad didn't.

"You're looking more and more like a girl every time I see you." Simon chortled, while Zaire closed his eyes. "You won't be able to hold onto Aaron looking like you do. He wants someone masculine; otherwise, he wouldn't be gay, you stupid hussy."

"Enough!"

Uma's voice startled Zaire, and he looked over Simon's shoulder to see several staff members, male and female, standing there. Simon turned, too, and Zaire saw when he paled at the audience.

"Either change your behaviour, Simon, or you'll be out. Zaire can dress and look however he wants to and will have the unwavering support of this school and many people in it. You and I had a conversation several months ago if you remember, and I told you to your face I was not interested. You have no say in who I have a relationship with. If you don't like it, leave."

Aaron's voice had Zaire swinging around to see him standing several steps to the side, an angry expression on his face. Zaire's heart raced at the number of people who had his back. He had never believed anyone would support his choices, but this show of people was almost more than his emotions could take. He swallowed hard against the tears, hoping they would stay locked away until he was in private.

"Fine. You will have my resignation on your desk tomorrow." Simon sneered at Zaire, looking him up and down, then pushed past him, stopping to the side of Aaron. "You'll regret choosing this…bitch," he growled, glaring at Zaire.

"Enough! Remove yourself from the property immediately. I do not need your resignation because you are fired with immediate effect. John, Ruth, please go with him and ensure he takes only what is his and leaves the property without issue."

Zaire knew what that meant. Aaron was concerned Simon would do something on his way out and wanted to reduce the chances of it. When the three had left, Zaire sagged back against the car, breathing hard.

"Are you okay, Zaire?" Uma's soft voice brought his gaze up to her concerned one, and he nodded. "I'm so glad I was near when he started."

"I wondered how you happened to be there."

"When I heard him yell at you, I got the attention of a few other people to make sure there were witnesses to whatever he did."

"I didn't do anything for him to say that. I—"

"Don't you dare blame yourself for what happened here."

Zaire flinched at the whip of Aaron's voice. He gazed over at Aaron, seeing him standing where he had been, clenching his fists. Zaire couldn't think of anything to answer with.

"That man—and I use the term very loosely— deserved everything he got. You are in no way to blame for anything that happened. Do you understand me?"

"Yes."

"Yes, what?"

Zaire's eyes widened as he knew what Aaron wanted. He glanced around, seeing people moving away from them now the drama was over.

"Well?"

Returning his gaze to Aaron, he saw barely leashed anger vibrating through his Daddy, and he could do nothing more than obey. Zaire shuffled over and wrapped his arms around Aaron's waist. "Yes, Daddy."

As close as he was to Aaron, he felt the shiver that went through him and arms enclosed him in a too-tight hug, but Zaire wouldn't complain. If Aaron needed this, Zaire would let him have it.

"God, I'm so sorry you had to deal with that asshole. But I'm so proud of you. Standing strong and not talking back to him, not denying who you are?" Aaron tilted Zaire's head back and cupped his jaw, pressing his lips against his in a brief kiss. "You are such a brave boy. My boy." He hesitated, searching

Zaire's face for something he must have found because he pressed another kiss to his lips and rested their foreheads together, whispering, "I love you, Zaire."

Tears overflowed, and he burrowed his face into his Daddy's neck. "I love you, too, Daddy. So much."

They stood there for a few moments before Aaron pulled away. "Let's go grab my things, and we can go home." Aaron held out his hand with a smile.

Zaire grinned and linked their fingers together.

↔

Zaire dropped into the booth seat, four days later, with a huge sigh of relief. That week had been easier once he became a bit more confident in himself, but the school environment hadn't been completely welcoming. Several members of staff ignored him when he spoke unless there was no other option, but most of them were welcoming and didn't say a word about his clothing choices.

"Long day, huh?" Nora commented.

Zaire lifted his head from the back of the seat and half-smiled at her. "Long week." He chuckled half-heartedly.

"I know what that feels like," she replied.

"When does Geoff get back?"

She sighed. "In three days. God, I miss him when he's gone."

Geoff occasionally worked away from home, and it was one of the reasons they had come out tonight.

Aaron had said Nora was moping and needed cheering up, so they had changed their plans of a night in to take her out instead. Zaire was tired, but he was determined to help Aaron distract her.

"He'll be home before you know it," Cord said, squeezing her shoulder.

"Do you like to dance?" Zaire asked her.

"Yeah."

"Come on." He slipped out of the booth and held out his hand. "Let's dance."

Zaire had no idea how long they had been dancing before he needed to sit down. They returned to the booth, seeing Rod and Delia had joined their group. Aaron slid out of his seat and let Zaire sit next to Delia, pulling out a stool to sit on instead and passed Zaire a bottle of water. Zaire grinned at him and drank half of it in one go.

"Thank you, Daddy."

"You're welcome."

"Zaire?" Rod's voice interrupted their mutual staring contest. "We have something to tell you. Two things, actually."

Zaire twisted in his seat to face his friend. "What's that?"

Rod looked at Delia and wrapped an arm around her shoulder, pulling her close. "Delia's pregnant."

"Oh my god! That's great news, guys!" He leaned forward and pulled them both into a hug.

"That's not all."

Zaire pulled back, narrowing his gaze. "It's not twins, is it? Because it would serve you right," he joked.

Delia laughed and punched his arm. "No, asshole."

"We got engaged, too," Rod said.

"Wow, you two have been busy." Zaire hugged them again and pulled back. "I'm so happy for you!"

"Congratulations to you both," Aaron said, holding out his hand. Rod shook it and thanked him.

Zaire knew he didn't want kids for himself, but he knew he'd be the best uncle in the world to them. He looked to Aaron, knowing he would spoil the kid rotten.

They spent the next few hours dancing, drinking, celebrating and commiserating in equal measures until Aaron declared it was time for them to go home. Zaire was secretly grateful for the news because he was shattered and wanted to sleep. As Aaron draped his jacket around Zaire's shoulders and snuggled him close, Zaire let out a contented sigh.

"See you guys soon," Aaron said, and Zaire waved at the table's occupants.

He woke when the car door opening made him jump.

"Sorry, I was trying to be quiet."

Zaire rubbed his eyes and realised they were at Aaron's house, which felt more like home than his own did. "It's okay. Sorry, I must've been tired."

"You're still tired. I'm taking you inside to bed, my sweet boy." Aaron helped Zaire out of the car and into the house, removing Zaire's shoes and coat for him. "Come on." They climbed the stairs, and Aaron led them to the bedroom. After quickly stripping Zaire and slipping a teddy over his head, Aaron pulled back the covers and tucked Zaire in. Sliding in behind, he spooned Zaire and rested a hand over his waist.

"Daddy?"

"Yes, sweetheart?"

"Can we go to the zoo tomorrow?"

"We'll see."

"Daddy?"

"Yes?"

"Can we find a cuddly toy for Rod and Delia's baby, too?"

"I don't see why not. Get some sleep."

"Daddy?"

Aaron chuckled, the exhale warm on the back of Zaire's neck. "Yes, Zaire?"

"I love you." Zaire threaded their fingers together and pulled Aaron's hand as close as he could.

"Love you, too, sweet boy."

FIVE MONTHS LATER

AARON

Aaron watched Zaire as he stood at the front of the assembly, reading the afternoon story to all the children. He was a natural and had everyone's attention, including staff. Zaire made the story come alive by using different voices and, occasionally, props. It made the children ask for him more often than not when they had the choice of narrator.

Zaire was now fully employed with the school after a long discussion between Aaron and the governors, who agreed Zaire could work there as long as any decisions needing to be made, which affected Zaire in any way, would be done jointly with the deputy headteacher. They wanted to ensure they couldn't be pointed at for favouritism. As soon as permission had been granted, Zaire had left the agency and joined the school full time one month ago, doing what he loved in Uma's class.

When Zaire finished the story, the children cheered, and he took a bow, his face beaming. Aaron strode up to the front and slid an arm around his shoulder, squeezing. "You're amazing," he whispered in Zaire's ear before turning to the children. "Wasn't that great?" The children responded with a loud affirmative. "Well, we can't do any better than that, so we are going to finish there. Please wait until your class teacher is ready before you stand. Good afternoon, children."

"Good afternoon, Mr Brown. Good afternoon, teachers."

Aaron realised he still had his arm around Zaire, and he removed it, though he didn't want to. "Are you okay?"

"Yep," Zaire confirmed with a grin.

"Any plans for this afternoon?" Aaron asked. They had not seen each other because Zaire had been at his mum's house over the weekend and had driven straight to school from her house that morning.

"Nope."

"Would you like to come round? I have a surprise for you." He didn't need to offer the enticement, but he did anyway.

"I'll be there. As always."

"Good. Don't take too long. You have a key. Use it if I'm not back before you."

"Yes," he looked around and whispered, "Daddy."

"Good boy."

With a wink, Aaron pivoted and left Zaire there. If he hadn't, he wouldn't have let him go back to the classroom and do his job. He would've taken him to his office and done things that would have gotten him fired. Two days and three nights without him was too long. Once in his office, he set to work, getting some paperwork finished. He needed something to take his mind off his boy.

Zaire's car was present when he arrived home, and he called for him when he entered the house. Quick footsteps sounded, and soon he was engulfed in his boy's arms as Zaire jumped up against him. Aaron laughed and wrapped an arm around his waist and under his hips as he walked further into the house.

"I missed you, sweet boy." He kissed him as he had wanted to do all day, demanding entry to Zaire's mouth and exploring the warm, wet area. Their tongues duelled as they fought to get closer to each other. Aaron turned and pressed Zaire against a wall, not wanting to hurt either of them by continuing to walk when he had his eyes closed from the pleasure of Zaire's mouth. Their hips thrust, their hardening cocks sliding together. Zaire's hands were in Aaron's hair, holding tight as moans left him.

They finally pulled away, gasping for air, and Aaron nuzzled his nose along Zaire's jaw and neck until he reached his favourite place. His teeth gained purchase on the area between his neck and shoulder, and he sucked—hard—marking Zaire where his skin was exposed with the off-the-shoulder jumper.

Zaire groaned, and his hips thrust harder against Aaron. "Daddy! Please. I need you."

Knowing his boy as he did now, Aaron reached a hand down and undid his trousers, pushing the fabric out of the way and slipping his hand between the satin and skin, gripping his cock.

"Oh! Daddy! Please!"

"I know, sweet boy. I've got you." Aaron pumped his hand, stroking up and down and twisting at the top, all the while kissing Zaire and muffling his moans and groans. Zaire's hips increased in speed, and Aaron knew he would not last much longer. He tightened his grip and kissed up to Zaire's ear. "Come for Daddy."

"Ah! Oh, fuck! I'm…" Zaire's cock released over Aaron's hand and no doubt over both their clothes, but he didn't care. All he cared about was the blissed-out look on Zaire's face as he regained his breathing.

Aaron brought his hand up and licked off the come from his fingers, watching Zaire's eyes dilate further at his actions. Once his hand was clean, he rested his hand under Zaire's ass and lifted him away from the wall. He carried him up the stairs to the bedroom and dropped him on the bed to Zaire's laughter.

Aaron stripped everything off and watched as Zaire got with the programme and did the same. When they were both naked, Aaron crawled over Zaire and took his mouth. His cock ached painfully and needed relief in the only place he could get it—with Zaire. Pulling away briefly to grab the lube, he slicked himself and settled between Zaire's legs. They had done away with condoms a couple of months earlier and nothing felt better than being bare inside Zaire.

He pressed his cock against Zaire's hole and surged forward, and as he seated himself fully inside his boy, he leaned down and kissed him reverently. Zaire began wriggling underneath him, indicating he was ready for more, and Aaron withdrew and thrust, groaning with the feel of Zaire's inner warmth. After being so long without him—three days was a long time to him—he knew they wouldn't last long, so he didn't mess around. His hips pistoned as Zaire wrapped his legs around Aaron's back, and Aaron slid his arms around Zaire's back. They were as close as they could be, and the position must have been right because Zaire whimpered and gripped Aaron's neck tightly.

"Fuck, my sweet, sweet boy. I'm there. Ah!" Aaron's hips stuttered, and before he released, he felt Zaire tense and a flood of warmth between them as Zaire's ass clenched on his cock. "Fuck!"

They stayed there for several breath-heaving moments before Aaron pulled back after a quick kiss. He stood and fetched a cloth from the bathroom, cleaning them both and settling next to Zaire to pull him into a hug.

"God, I missed you."

"I missed you, too, Daddy."

"How was it?"

Zaire was quiet for a moment, and Aaron allowed him time to collect his thoughts. "It was embarrassing as hell but also cathartic. At least we don't need to hide from her now."

Zaire had visited his mother so he could explain their relationship to her. As he said, he hadn't wanted to be someone different when we were with her, so he'd wanted to tell her everything their relationship involved. Aaron had been surprised but overwhelmingly proud of how far Zaire had come since they'd met.

"How did she take it?" Aaron brushed his fingers through Zaire's hair.

"It took a bit of explaining, hence the embarrassment, but she understood by the end. She doesn't understand why we need it, but she understands we do."

"That's all we need her to. Nobody needs to understand us; just accept us. I'm glad you'll be able to be yourself when you see her."

Chuckling, Zaire said, "Are we really talking about my mother when we are naked on your bed and after doing what we did?"

Aaron laughed, then sobered. "Our."

"What?"

"Our bed." Zaire lifted his head to look at Aaron, a question in his eyes. "I'd like you to move in if you want to."

A brilliant smile crossed his face, and he moved, straddling Aaron and resting his hands either side of his head. "Really, Daddy? Really?"

The child-like excitement was contagious, and Aaron grinned as he slid his hands up Zaire's back. "Really. Truly. Honestly."

"Yes, please, Daddy." Zaire pressed kisses all over his face. "Yes, yes, yes!"

"I'll take it as a yes, shall I?" Aaron laughed.

"Hell, yes!"

Aaron stilled Zaire's movements and locked gazes. "I love you, sweet boy."

"I love you, Daddy."

⟵⟶

ZAIRE

Zaire thought back to the conversation he'd had with his mother. It had been one of the most embarrassing moments of Zaire's life, but it needed to happen. His mother had been such an important person in Zaire's life, and now Zaire was embracing both sides of himself, he wanted to ensure he could do so in his mother's company, too.

After the initial explanation and question session about what their kind of relationship was, his mother had agreed, although she didn't understand it, she would never turn him away from it. She made him laugh throughout the weekend with small questions here and there, but she'd hit the nail on the head with one of them.

"Do you think the need to be…free from responsibility has come about because of what happened with your dad?"

Zaire thought about her words and realised the truth to them. "Yes. Whenever my thoughts head in the direction of what happened and what he did, I find myself getting stressed and wanting to hide away from everything. Being a boy helps me to let go of everything for a short time and forget what happened. It allows my brain a chance to recover, rest and rejuvenate, so I can think like a grown-up again."

"I'm so sorry for everything that happened with him. I tried to shield you from it as best as I could. But when he got worse, I did the only thing I knew would work."

Zaire and his mother had a complete heart to heart, and everything was finally settled. He felt much better about the situation, and it was made even better by the arrival of Car. His brother, whom he hadn't seen in around a year, had turned up out of the blue—at least to Zaire, his mother had known—and they'd had a fantastic weekend of reconnecting.

He would have loved to have involved Zena, but he didn't think she would ever forgive him for what she saw as being his fault—breaking up their parents. He may try reconnecting at some point but not right now.

Next weekend, he was taking Aaron to see his mother, and he was excited about it.

Almost as excited as he had been when Aaron had announced he could start at the school again if he wanted to. He'd jumped at the chance as soon as Aaron had explained the rules behind it. Uma had been happy to see him, and Zaire happy to be back with the children again.

Now, he lived as a whole person rather than hiding

part of him away. Or at least he was trying. He dressed how he wanted, although he had realised skirts were not the best thing to wear when he would be up and down climbing frames and playing with the kids. He stuck to trousers from then on. He'd even begun wearing natural makeup. There had been some upset about what he wore, to begin with, and some parents had made complaints, but Aaron had arranged a parent's evening so it could be addressed. In his usual straightforward way, he had explained, in no uncertain terms, what was expected of the parents of the school. Questions were asked and answered, and from that moment, no issues were raised.

Occasionally, his old fears came to the forefront when they were going somewhere new, but Aaron was always there with him in that situation. He never left Zaire to face it alone.

Zaire would never be able to tell Aaron how much he appreciated everything Aaron had done for him. He had literally changed Zaire's life for the better in every perceivable way.

Aaron loved him, and he loved Aaron. What more could he ask for?

Have you read the Daddy/little book from the Crush series? Love Scene is Book 8 but can be read as a standalone.

Sign up to my newsletter to get a free Crush

prequel short story, Love Conquers and a serial newsletter story every month.

If you have a moment, would you write a review for Spoil Me, Daddy please? Reviews help other readers decide whether they would like to read the book, and therefore, are also important for authors.

ABOUT ELOUISE EAST

I am Elouise East but feel free to call me Elli. I write sweet and steamy connections in gay romance. I also touch on taboo stories under the name Elouise R East.

Books that tell the stories where friendship and family are the focal point - be it blood family or chosen - is very important to me. That's why I include a variety of personalities, talents, ages, situations and abilities as I believe a story needs, or a character needs. I want my characters to be real, to be relatable, to be free to have whatever views they tell me they have. And trust me, most of the time, I do not have *any* say in the matter!

My characters come to life on the page for me as well as my readers. Their stories unfold in front of me, and I have very little input into how they want to be shown. Just like real life, the lives of my characters change with every choice, every interaction and every conversation. And I wouldn't have it any other way.

I write books that are emotionally realistic, even if liberties are taken with other aspects of my stories. I don't know any other way to write. It comes from deep inside.

Who am I? A single parent to two children who

make life worth living. An avid reader who still devours every book she can get her hands on. A student of learning about any subject that takes her fancy. An author of books she would read herself. And a romantic at heart who loves anything cheesy.

Who's in?

———————————————

Stalk me here… ;-)
https://elouiseeast.com/
https://elouiseeast.com/newsletter
https://linktr.ee/elouiseeastauthor

Check out https://elouiseeast.com/books for my books!

BOOKS BY ELOUISE EAST

<u>DADDY</u>

Love Me, Daddy

Soothe Me, Daddy

Spoil Me, Daddy

<u>CRUSH</u>

First Kiss

Instant Desire

Primary Seduction

Deep Down

A Crush for Christmas

Life Support

Covert Strength

Love Scene

Lawful Attraction

CLUB ROYAL

Royal Firsts

Rogue Royal

Secretive Royal

Grieving Royal

Disowned Royal

Trained Royal

Awakened Royal

Commanding Royal

LOVE IN FLAMES

Out of the Frying Pan

Smokescreen

Breathing Fire

JUST A LITTLE CRUSH

Star-Crossed

He's Behind You

A Special Love (newsletter story)

DARK & DIVERGENT

A Biker Make Three

Forbidden Temptation

Too Many Secrets

STANDALONE

Treehouse Whispers

9 781915 638311